Praise for the Red Carpet Catering Mystery Series

MURDER ON A DESIGNER DIET (#3)

"The Red Carpet Catering series delivers a buffet of appealing characters, irresistible movie-industry details, and tantalizing plot twists. As delicious as a gourmet meal—and leaves you hungry for more!"

– Susan O'Brien,
Agatha Award-Nominated Author of *Finding Sky*

"Movie lovers, this is your book! Engaging and high-spirited, Penelope Sutherland never expected that catering for the cast and crew of a top flight movie would lead to...murder. Great fun."

– Terrie Farley Moran,
Agatha Award-Winning Author of *Caught Read-Handed*

MURDER ON THE HALF SHELL (#2)

"With a nice island flavor, a nice puzzling mystery and a great cast of characters, this was a very enjoyable read."

– *Dru's Book Musings*

"A fast-paced cozy easily read and enjoyed in an afternoon...with Simmons' picturesque writing style you can almost taste the salt in the air. Take a vacation and join Penelope."

– *The Reading Room*

"Such a fun book..The characters are very likable and the writing is very well-done. Think of it as a cozy behind the scenes."

– *Booklikes*

MURDER ON A SILVER PLATTER (#1)

"Delicious! A great read written by someone who knows the behind the scenes world of filmmaking...A winner!"

– Kathryn Leigh Scott,
Author of the Jinx Fogarty Mysteries

"Loved this book! The characters are well-drawn and it's cleverly plotted. Totally engrossing...I felt as though I was actually on a movie set. The author is well-versed in her setting and she is able to keep the reader in suspense. I can't wait for the second book in the series."

– Marianna Heusler,
Edgar-Nominated Author

"Much of what makes this such an enjoyable new mystery is the background information on both catering and movie-making. Equally compelling is just how seamlessly author Simmons works Penelope into the investigation...this is a fun new series for readers who enjoy their theatrical showbiz mysteries with a culinary twist."

– *Kings River Life Magazine*

"With a likeable cast of characters and an inside look at the movie industry, this was an equally entertaining and engaging debut."

– *Dru's Book Musings*

"Simmons has given us quite a good beginning to a new series; she manages to create characters that are both believable and likable, while weaving in small tidbits of movie-making and what is involved in catering food to a movie crew. I look forward to reading the next in the series. Highly recommended."

– *Any Good Book*

MURDER
ON A
DESIGNER
DIET

**The Red Carpet Catering Mystery Series
by Shawn Reilly Simmons**

MURDER
ON A
DESIGNER
DIET

A RED CARPET CATERING MYSTERY

SHAWN REILLY
SIMMONS

HENERY PRESS

MURDER ON A DESIGNER DIET
A Red Carpet Catering Mystery
Part of the Henery Press Mystery Collection

First Edition | June 2016

Henery Press, LLC
www.henerypress.com

Trade Paperback ISBN-13: 978-1-63511-033-3
Digital epub ISBN-13: 978-1-63511-034-0
Kindle ISBN-13: 978-1-63511-035-7
Hardcover Paperback ISBN-13: 978-1-63511-036-4

Printed in the United States of America

For Ildy

ACKNOWLEDGMENTS

First and foremost, I must thank everyone in my family for their constant love and support, and tolerance of my crazy work schedule. You allow me the time I need to write and plot, and otherwise spend a lot of time in my imaginary worlds.

Thanks to Stephanie Biasi for letting me crash on her couch while researching different locations in Manhattan for the book. And a special thanks for making those soft shell crabs for dinner I still think about today.

A huge thanks goes out to all of my readers and fans, and the incredibly supportive mystery-writing community. Your encouragement means the world to me and I can't thank you enough. Without you, none of this would be possible.

Thanks to one of my earliest supporters, Dru Ann Love. Her enthusiasm for the books has been a source of inspiration for me from the very beginning.

My undying gratitude and thanks go to Kendel Lynn, Art Molinares and everyone at Henery Press for their constant support and guidance. My editors, Rachel Jackson and Erin George, are two of the most insightful and positive people I've ever met, and I'm grateful beyond words for everything they do for me.

And I'd like to thank all of the chefs and caterers I've met and worked with over the years. They've come from all walks of life, with such varied backgrounds and personalities, all bringing their individuality to something we all understand. Food brings people together, helps us express our love for one another, sustains us and inspires us. I'm honored to have known each and every one of you.

And of course, to Matthew and Russell, my everything.

CHAPTER 1

"We have to move if we're going to make time," Penelope yelled over her shoulder to her crew as she swiped her forehead with the sleeve of her chef coat. She shifted her weight back and forth, bouncing slightly on the thick rubber floor mat of the kitchen as she worked, her blond ponytail damp and sticking to the back of her neck.

"What's going up first, Boss?" Francis called to her from behind, his back turned as he worked over the flames leaping up through the grill grate.

Penelope glanced at the ancient clock hung on the dingy white tiles of the old hotel's basement kitchen. "Let's take it all up at once. We can use their pan racks." She eyed the tall carts against the wall, their multi-level slots full of empty sheet pans, and hoped they were relatively clean.

"Sure, Boss, no problem." Francis flipped the steaks in front of him, turning them quickly to ensure they cooked evenly. The New York strips sizzled loudly on the grates.

Penelope bent back over her cauliflower au gratin on the large stainless steel prep table. She faced the service window where the wait staff would normally come to pick up finished plates and take them to the hotel's guests in the small restaurant upstairs. But today The Crawford was closed to the public, about to undergo a major renovation, and rented out beforehand to their film crew. It was Red Carpet Catering's first day on set and principal filming had just begun at the historic hotel near the High Line in Manhattan.

"Remember to keep those steaks under," Penelope warned

Francis. "They'll come the rest of the way up to temp while they're resting."

Francis nodded, keeping his eyes on the grill. The bandana tied around his head had turned dark red in the hot basement. He began pulling the finished steaks from the flames.

"Open the oven for me, would you?" Penelope said, picking up the large sheet pan her individual ramekins of au gratin were resting on. She turned around carefully in the tight space between them, her forearms straining from the weight of the pan. She slid them into the oven, careful not to spill any over the sides.

Penelope closed the oven door and poked the steaks with her finger, checking for doneness. "These are perfect." She glanced down the kitchen to the cold station where the rest of her team was working. They were putting the finishing touches on the salads, assembling a dessert display, and garnishing a carving station that held three roasted whole chickens with sprigs of fresh parsley.

Penelope shouted over the din of the industrial exhaust fans on the back wall, "Get those cakes in cold storage as soon as you can. It's way too hot in here to keep them out."

"What?" her assistant chef yelled, cupping his hand to his ear.

Penelope sighed and walked closer to him, still raising her voice so he could hear her. "I said, it's hot in here. Get a move on and put those desserts away before they melt. We'll come back down for them when they're halfway through lunch."

Penelope watched him plate the last few slices of cake and wished again there was a window in the stuffy room. She hoped whoever was renovating the hotel would remember to include a proper ventilation system for the chefs who normally worked in this kitchen. She gathered up the empty cake boxes and tossed them into the trash while her assistant placed their desserts in the walk-in refrigerator.

Penelope went back to the oven to check on her cauliflower dish. A wave of heat hit her in the face when she opened the door and saw the crocks of cheesy cauliflower were bubbling, but none of them were brown on top.

"This broiler is out," she yelled to Francis, who was pulling the last two well-done steaks from the grill.

Francis cursed in response. They looked up at the clock on the wall at the same time and saw they only had five minutes until they were scheduled to serve lunch to the cast and crew.

"Okay, watch out," Penelope said, grabbing two dish towels and pulling the hot sheet pan out of the oven. She placed it on top of the stove and eased the door shut with her steel-toed boot. There were several drawers tucked up underneath the service counter and she pulled one out, quickly ransacking through the kitchen tools.

"Help me find a torch, would you?"

Francis turned and pulled open the farthest drawer, which screeched loudly on its rollers. He picked through a few of the tools, then closed it and pulled open the next one. "Here you go, Boss." He held up a butane kitchen torch.

Penelope took it from him. "Is the igniter in there?"

"Yep," Francis said, handing her a round silver sparker.

"I hope it has fuel," Penelope muttered. She twisted the valve on the side of the torch and clicked the igniter a few times. Finally a thin blue flame shot out of the spout. "Don't you love working in someone else's kitchen?" She turned back to her dish. She waved the torch in even strokes over the first crock, watching the cheese and breadcrumbs toast under the flame. "Only forty-nine to go," she said under her breath as she moved to the next one.

The walkie-talkie inside the pocket of her chef coat crackled and she paused a moment to pull it out. A staticky voice buzzed, "Five...catering...go...lunch."

Penelope looked at the radio for a second and then pushed the button on the side. "Say again, I didn't hear that."

"Five...not...Stephens...lunch," the voice said.

Penelope sighed. "I can barely make out what you're saying. You're breaking up and it's loud down here. Stephens wants lunch in five? Is that right?" Penelope said. She cut her eyes at Francis who stood next to her admiring his steak platter. He shook his head at her in response.

"Stephens...another...upstairs," the voice said, fading out at the end.

"This radio is a piece of crap," Penelope said, tossing it onto the counter and getting back to work with the torch.

"Why don't you call him?" Francis asked. "Who is it, the AD? What's his name?"

"I don't remember, actually," Penelope said, glancing again at the radio. "I don't like to call the crew in case they're rolling and they haven't turned off their phones. Wouldn't want to ruin a shot and get someone in trouble. Plus I only get one bar down here." She looked up at the clock again. "This is when we're supposed to roll setup upstairs and everything is almost ready. Let's stick to the schedule."

"Okay, Boss. Hey, you guys," Francis bellowed over the fans. "We're rolling in one minute." He pulled the tall carts around to the front of the service station and they filled them up, careful not to jostle the food too much as they loaded everything.

Penelope watched them out of the corner of her eye while she worked. When she'd toasted her last gratin, she brought her sheet pan around and slid it onto one of the lower shelves. "That's still a little hot. Be careful when you wrap them."

Francis began looping clear plastic wrap around one of the carts, passing the roll to another chef and back again until both racks were completely covered, the food protected inside.

Penelope retrieved the radio from the countertop. "This is catering. We're heading up."

A click and static was the only response. She sighed and punched the button to call the service elevator to the basement. The rest of the crew was upstairs, with principal filming taking place in the penthouse suite.

This movie was a small independent production, and they'd be feeding about fifty crew members on any given day. Or at least that's what Penelope had been told when she'd signed on to the project. Experience had taught her that production schedules, crews, and even actors could change at any time during a movie, so she had learned to be flexible, even if doing so took her out of her comfort zone.

The elevator doors slowly rolled open, the musty moving blankets lining the walls swaying lazily as it came to a stop. Penelope reminded herself not to lean up against them.

"There's nothing creepier than an abandoned hotel," Francis said under his breath.

"It's not abandoned, just empty. But you're right about it being creepy," Penelope agreed.

After Penelope and her crew had all squeezed inside, the doors rumbled slowly closed and the elevator slowly groaned upward.

CHAPTER 2

The next morning, Penelope set a plate down in front of Arlena, who sat with her arms folded across her chest at their kitchen island. Arlena stared down into a pair of matching egg yolks.

"Go ahead and eat it. You know you want to." Sam nudged Arlena's bicep with his elbow.

"But I don't want to, that's the point," Arlena said. She gazed at the sunny side up eggs a few beats more, then picked up her fork and pierced them, releasing their gooey goodness onto the buttery home fries and toast beneath.

"I'll eat it if you don't want it," Sam said, taking an enthusiastic bite from his identical plate.

"No," Penelope scolded. "I promised I'd help her get ready, but she's got to eat the food herself."

Arlena dropped her fork and perched her thin elbows on the countertop. Dropping her head into her hands, she said, "Remind me why I'm doing this again?"

Penelope glanced at Sam and said, "You want the part, so you have to look the part. That's what you said, and that means putting on the weight. Cold eggs taste terrible. Dig in."

Penelope normally made things like green smoothies or egg white frittatas for breakfast. She was Arlena's live-in chef and best friend, and she always cooked for Arlena and Sam on the mornings they were home. They were both busy actors, and a lot of the time they were on film sets, so Penelope looked forward to the mornings they were home together.

Penelope opened the cover of a three-ring binder on the counter and flipped through the first few pages. "The nutritionist says you have to hit at least four thousand calories a day for the next six weeks to bulk up. She's got it all planned out here."

Arlena groaned. "I know, I know...fine. I'll do it." She scooped some egg and toast into her mouth.

"After breakfast you'll only have a little over three thousand calories to go," Penelope said, scanning a few of the suggested meal plans.

"I have no idea how I'm going to manage that," Arlena said between bites.

"You can do it, babe," Sam said, a bit of egg yolk staining the corner of his mouth. "It'll be easy once you get in the habit of eating more."

Arlena rolled her eyes and took another bite. "I swear I don't starve myself to stay thin. You both know how much I love good food. I only try to be as healthy as I can."

Penelope looked up from the binder. "The nutritionist doesn't want to create any lingering health problems, so she's kept your diet plan on the clean side. We just have to up your calories in the healthiest way possible. Lots of shakes, extra carbs."

Sam took a triangle of toast and mopped up the remaining egg yolk from his plate. "How much weight are you trying to put on?"

"At least twenty-five pounds," Arlena said quietly, not looking up from her plate.

"Twenty-five pounds?" Sam asked. "You're going to look great."

"We'll see," Arlena said skeptically.

"What's the part again?" Sam asked.

"Well, if I even get the part, I'll be playing a music teacher from Indiana who ends up getting a group of her students to Carnegie Hall for a competition."

"And you have to put on weight for that?" Sam asked, leaning his back against his stool and stretching his arm behind Arlena's chair.

"It's based on a true story. The woman looks like me, kind of, but more full-figured. My agent thinks I'll have a better shot if I can show I'm able to change physically."

"You're doing a *Raging Bull*," Penelope said, still leafing through the binder, reminding herself to pick up some of the suggested groceries on the list.

"I'm going for *Monster*," Arlena said, eating another bite of toast. She'd almost cleaned her plate.

"No, you're more like *Bridget Jones*," Sam said. "You're not mean enough for *Monster*."

"Oh yeah? Force me to eat greasy breakfasts every day for a month and you'll see how much of a monster I can be." Arlena pushed her plate away, just a few scraps of toast lying in a puddle of egg yolk remaining.

Sam pulled Arlena off of her stool and into his lap, hugging her tightly. "It doesn't matter what size you are. To me, you are perfect." He kissed her sweetly on the cheek. Arlena hugged him back, her mood lightening.

"Are you coming with us tonight?" Arlena asked a couple hours later as Penelope came through the back door into the kitchen. She had just gotten back from a run, her cheeks red and her shirt damp with sweat under her light jacket.

"What's tonight again?" she asked as she pulled a bottle of water from the refrigerator.

Arlena flipped through a few envelopes. The vanilla protein shake Penelope had mixed for her before she left sweated on the countertop, a blue straw pointed towards her face.

"Max's thing. The fashion show in Chelsea. You're not working, are you?"

"No, we're off this weekend, not due back until Monday. This new job is making me so tired, I forgot about tonight. For some reason I thought the show was next weekend."

Arlena pulled a shiny black card with an ornate letter *S*

embossed in the center from their stack of mail and held it up. "No, it's tonight." She waved the card at Penelope. "It's Sienna's New York debut."

"Right, I remembered that part." They'd met Sienna the previous summer in Florida while they worked on a movie with her then-fiancé, Gavin McKenna. "Shoot, I have to call Joey. I know I told him the wrong day," Penelope said, looking around the kitchen for her phone. It was gleaming silver on the far granite countertop. She picked it up and saw that she had a missed call from him and a text that read: *We still on for tonight? NYC?*

"It looks like he remembered. Now I feel like a crazy person," Penelope said, calling him back. "Great, voicemail. Hey, Joey, it's Penny. Call me when you can about tonight."

"Good," Arlena said. "Max is excited that we're all coming, especially Daddy."

Arlena and Max's father, the legendary actor Randall Madison, was in town visiting between film projects.

Penelope nodded and finished her bottle of water. "I didn't know Max was that into fashion, or modeling." She pulled out the refuse compartment next to the sink and slipped the bottle into the recycling bin.

Arlena shrugged, distracted by another piece of mail. "Max is into a lot of things. He and Sienna have become good friends since we were in Florida. Gavin too. I know he wants to help her out. He's got name recognition, and he does wear clothes well, so that should be helpful to her."

"What am I going to wear?" Penelope looked down at her running shorts and dirty sneakers. Her legs were salty with sweat and she hadn't shaved in a couple of days. Fine blond stubble shimmered on her kneecaps.

"Well, not that." Arlena eyed Penelope up and down. "Come over to my side of the house later and we'll find something."

"Thanks," Penelope said.

Her phone rang and she glanced down to see Joey's name flash on the screen over a picture of the two of them together on the roof of Rockefeller Center, the Manhattan skyline fogged in behind them, skyscrapers poking through the gray clouds. She smiled and pulled the phone up to her ear, answering on the way upstairs to her room.

CHAPTER 3

Penelope's fingers were entwined with Joey's much thicker ones as he led her through the crowd of flashing bulbs towards the heavy wooden door of the nightclub. Dozens of photographers were lined up on either side of red velvet ropes, clicking their shutters rapidly as they passed. A few of them pulled the cameras away from their faces for a better look at her and Joey, then looked past them expectantly down the red carpet for someone they recognized.

A thin young man in a butler's uniform and white gloves pulled open the door of the old church as they approached. Penelope could see a large crowd of people milling around inside the nightclub, glasses of wine and cocktails in their hands. Just then she heard a frenzy of shouting and saw the night sky light up with flashes as Arlena, Sam, and Randall walked down the carpet. They paused to pose for the photographers, Arlena flanked by the two men she loved the most. Arlena wore a pale silk dress and bright red high-heeled sandals, her long black hair spilling over her shoulders in shiny waves.

Joey placed his hand at the small of Penelope's back as they entered the club. "I know I said it earlier, but you look beautiful, Penny Blue."

Penelope thanked him and looked down at the little black dress she had chosen from Arlena's closet. It showed much more leg than she was normally comfortable with, but Arlena insisted it looked perfect on her. Penelope reached up and straightened the knot of Joey's tie and smoothed down his collar. "I'm glad you're here. I wasn't sure if tonight would be your idea of fun."

Joey laughed. "I'm not the most fashionable guy, I guess. But I love being with you. You want a cocktail or a glass of wine?" He nodded toward the bar.

Penelope paused a moment then said, "A dirty martini, please."

"A fancy drink for my girl tonight. Two dirty martinis, please," he said to the bartender, raising his voice to be heard over the crowd.

Penelope looked at the side of Joey's face as he ordered, admiring his strong jaw. He'd just said he loved being with her. It wasn't the same as saying he loved her, but it was close. Penelope's heart skipped when she thought about Joey. A lot of times she'd catch herself thinking about him while she was working, chopping vegetables or standing at the grill, her thoughts wandering to the last time they were together or something funny he'd said. They'd been seeing each other for the better part of a year and maybe, quite possibly even, she could be in love with him. But she was too afraid to say it first for fear it would scare him off or put her in a weakened position in their relationship. She didn't want to think about the possibility of telling Joey she loved him and him not saying it back.

"There you guys are," Arlena said as she and the others joined them at the bar. "I never even saw you after we got out of the limo." Sam moved closer to the bar and shouted over the crowd to order drinks.

"I've never been here," Joey said. "Heard about it, of course." He looked up at the vaulted ceiling. The nightclub had originally been a church, a Gothic Revival brownstone built in the early nineteenth century. It had been deconsecrated, sold by the diocese, and converted into a private drug rehab center in the 1960s. Then in the early '70s, it was bought by the son of a wealthy Greek family and turned into a nightclub, one of many he owned around the world, all in former houses of worship. Xapa was a landmark in the

Manhattan nightlife scene, infamous for its celebrity clientele and free-flowing drug trade back in the day, although currently it was much tamer, attracting more tourist business than anything else.

Randall handed Arlena and Sam their cocktails. "I used to come here all the time," he said, taking a sip of his martini and nodding at the stage. "I saw Blondie for the first time right over there."

"Blondie?" Arlena asked distractedly. She took a sip of her drink, careful not to spill any on her sheer white dress.

"Arlena, you know who Blondie is, right?" Randall paused and stared at her.

"Oh yeah, she's cool," Arlena said evasively, looking out over the crowd. "I wonder where Max is."

Randall shook his head and sighed. "I'm sure he's backstage getting ready for the show."

The rear wall of the club was draped in heavy black velvet. Several giant disco balls dangled from the wooden beams above their heads, slowly rotating and tossing flashes of shimmery light around the room, landing briefly on the faces of the crowd below. There was a raised runway in the center of the club hugged by the same black velvet material that lined the walls, and rows of folding chairs lined up on either side. A few people had claimed their seats around the stage, but most of the crowd was still mingling with an expectant energy. Penelope could see movement just behind the curtains of the main stage where she assumed Sienna and her models were getting ready for the show.

"How long are you in town for, Sam?" Joey asked.

"I'm leaving tomorrow for Munich to get started on the next Sloan picture. We'll be there three weeks then move around to different countries like we always do."

Joey listened as Sam talked about the filming sites throughout Europe for his next action movie. "Then I'll be back here again in a few months for our premiere." He kissed Arlena on the cheek.

"What premiere?" Joey asked, finishing off his drink and glancing at the bartender.

"*Remember the Fall* is set to debut at the Empire Film Festival in the spring," Arlena said. "That's the movie where we all met. Oh God, I just realized I have no idea how big I'm going to be. If I get the Indiana part, I'll have to get all new clothes."

Joey looked at her with a questioning glance.

"She's putting on weight for a role," Penelope murmured in his ear as Arlena began discussing different dress sizes with Sam.

"Oh." He chuckled, glancing at Arlena's flat stomach and then averting his eyes quickly. "For a minute, I thought she was talking about something else."

Penelope shook her head. "She's just getting started, twenty-five pounds is her goal. Excuse me. I'm going to find the ladies' room before the show starts." A purple neon Venus symbol was hung from the ceiling in the back corner next to a flickering Mars, pointing to a darkened hallway. "Be right back."

At the end of the dark hallway, there were two doors, both etched with graffiti and plastered with bumper stickers of different bands. She could make out a large circle painted on each, but she had a hard time deciding which one was the female symbol. Looking over her shoulder, she saw she was alone in the hallway, no one approaching to give her a clue about which door to use.

Penelope chose the door on the left, pressing the cold greasy paint with her fingertips. She didn't see anyone inside, so she quickly made her way to the bank of sinks and peeked under the stalls. Noticing a pair of men's shoes facing the toilet in the farthest one, she tiptoed back towards the door on her high heels.

Back in the hallway, she set her shoulders and entered the opposite room, breathing a sigh of relief after confirming she was alone in the women's bathroom. Quickly choosing a stall, she latched the door behind her.

Just as she began to hitch up her skirt, the bathroom door banged open. A spray of giggles followed, bouncing off of the porcelain tiles. They were joined by a deeper, more masculine laugh. Penelope heard the latch slide closed on the bathroom door, locking them all inside together.

"What the...?" Penelope whispered to herself. She pulled her skirt back down and stood frozen in the stall, strands of discarded toilet paper curling around her high heels. The sounds of kissing followed more giggles and then soft moaning from the couple on the other side of the stall.

Penelope peered through the crack in the door and saw the back of a tall man with shoulder-length blond hair and a woman's thin legs anchored at his waist as she sat on the counter, kissing him hungrily and running her hands through his hair.

"Ouch," he said, laughing, as the woman tried to untangle a lock of his hair from her large jade ring. As the sounds of their kissing and groping became more intense, Penelope decided to let them know they weren't alone before things progressed any further. She cleared her throat loudly.

The amorous couple either hadn't heard her over their moans or didn't care that they weren't alone. Penelope looked again and saw the man's face in the mirror. Clearly he only had his girlfriend on his mind, his eyes closed to the rest of the world. Penelope rolled her eyes and cleared her throat again, louder this time. The man finally paused. "Did you hear something?" His voice was deep and he had an accent, but Penelope couldn't place its origin. He was tan and gorgeous, that much she could tell.

"Hear what?" the woman said breathily, kissing his neck.

Penelope turned and flushed the toilet behind her.

The man pulled away from her and let out a deep-throated laugh. "We should have checked to make sure we were alone. Let's go." He quickly slid her off of the counter and onto her feet, rushing her towards the door. Penelope tried to get a look at her but only caught a glimpse of her long blond hair, twisted with strands of purple and green highlights, from behind his broad shoulders as he unlatched the door.

They hurried out of the bathroom after the man peeked out to make sure the hallway was empty. The door banged shut behind them. Penelope sighed, thankful to be alone again.

"There she is," Joey said, handing her a martini as she

returned to the bar. The lights dimmed and brightened three times.

"Looks like they're ready to start. Let's find our seats," Randall said.

As they walked towards the runway, they were met at the edge of the chairs by another hipster butler, this one with blue-black hair swept into an Elvis-style updo.

"Mr. Madison, Miss Madison, right this way." He led them down to the front row and indicated a group of seats in the center of the aisle. The lights dimmed and a large spotlight shone on the runway.

"Ladies and gentlemen, welcome to Sienna Wentworth's New York fashion debut. We hope you enjoy her collection entitled *Flesh and Bone*."

Murmurs from the crowd were drowned out by thumping electronic dance music. The curtain was pulled aside and the first model stepped out, sauntering down the runway. He kept pace with the music but walked in a casual, almost offhand way, his hips jutting forward as he gazed off to an imagined horizon over their heads. Another model followed close behind, and Penelope began to see the similarities in their clothes. Low-slung pants, sleeveless shirts with ragged slashes across the front revealing tan, clean-shaven torsos, and studded black leather belts crisscrossed at their waists. Their hair was sprayed into waves on one side of their heads and their eyes were rimmed in heavy black eyeliner. Diamond-studded dog collars pinched each of their necks, glinting in the lights as they passed by.

Penelope admired the colors and designs as they strolled past, thinking the clothes were well-constructed but, at the same time, wondering who would wear them. Penelope looked at Joey, who watched the show with interest, then put a hand to her mouth to suppress a laugh as she tried to picture him in a ripped t-shirt and skinny jeans.

After a few more models had walked the runway, the curtain opened again and Penelope sucked in her breath. It was the man from the bathroom, wearing a suit, the pants cut much tighter than the average businessman would wear. His dress shirt was unbuttoned to his waist, and his chest was heavy with muscle, an elaborate tattoo of interlocking crosses wrapping around his abdomen. Unlike the others, his hair was slicked back and he wore aviator sunglasses that reflected back the spotlights to the crowd. He smirked easily as he walked, adjusting the dog collar around his neck.

"Gordon Gekko for the new millennium," Joey murmured to Penelope as the model passed. An ornate *S* on the back of his jacket matched the one on Sienna's invitation.

Max was the next model to emerge from behind the curtain. He wore a suit also, dark blue and well-tailored. He walked confidently, though less smoothly than the other models. Pausing at the end of the runway, he pulled open his jacket, placing a hand on his waist. He paused a beat and strutted back, catching Penelope's eye and winking at her as he passed.

Penelope looked out of the corner of her eye at Joey. He either hadn't noticed or had no reaction to Max's flirtation.

When Max disappeared behind the curtain, the first model reemerged, quickly followed by the others in the order they had first appeared, the crowd clapping as they filed past. Eight of them lined the runway, four on each side, bowing to the applause. The curtains opened again and Sienna emerged, holding two gold leashes attached to the collars around the necks of the last two models, Max and the man from the bathroom.

The crowd rose to its feet as they walked to the end, Sienna stopping to take a bow, the leashes grasped at her sides. After a minute, the models began to walk again, filing back behind the curtain in a single line. Sienna, Max, and his partner model brought up the rear. Just before they disappeared behind the curtain, Max turned to wave at the crowd and Sienna playfully pulled on his leash. He laughed and ducked behind the curtain.

The lights rose and it took Penelope a few seconds for her eyes to adjust. She followed her friends over to the bar.

"What did you think?" Arlena asked.

"Cool clothes," Sam said. "But what's with the dog collars? I hope that's not a new trend costume designers will start making us wear."

"Not sure," Arlena said, tapping her fingernails on her martini glass. "We'll have to ask Sienna what she was trying to convey."

Randall chuckled. "I never thought I'd see the day Max would be put on a leash."

"Maybe she's commenting on gender roles," Penelope said. "We think it's funny, but if the roles were reversed...a lot of people would be offended if they saw female models on leashes being led around by a male designer."

"I was thinking the same thing," Joey said. "I figure she's trying to make a point about something, I just don't quite get it."

"Who cares?" Randall said, shaking his head. "The more important question is...who wants a drink?"

CHAPTER 4

"How did I do?" Max asked. He stood next to Randall, and Penelope noticed Max resembled his father even more than usual, each with their long hair slicked back. Max was a little shorter, but there was no mistaking they were father and son.

Max had changed into casual dress pants and a simple white shirt, but the diamond-studded dog collar still glittered around his neck. He held the neck of a beer bottle loosely between his fingers.

"You did good, kid," Randall said, patting him on the back.

"Thanks, Dad." He was much jitterier than usual, almost vibrating with excitement.

Hannah Devore sauntered up, tucked herself under Max's arm, and smiled shyly at the group. She was Max's girlfriend on his reality show, which sometimes bled over into real life. Penelope wasn't sure how they really felt about each other. Sometimes Max said their relationship was just a part of the show, but sometimes he talked about them doing things together outside of work.

"I didn't see you in the audience earlier, Hannah," Arlena said.

Hannah giggled and tucked a loose strand of blond hair back under her slouchy knit hat. "I was backstage, helping them get ready." She accepted a glass of white wine from Max. Penelope's stomach did a flip when she recognized the jade ring on Hannah's third finger. She'd seen it in the bathroom, entangled in another man's hair.

"Is that..." Penelope stammered, gazing at Hannah's ring. Pulling herself together, she continued, "Are those real diamonds?"

dragging her eyes from Hannah to Max and pretending to take a closer look at his dog collar.

"Yeah," Max said, with a note of disbelief. "Sienna had them custom made for the show. I get to keep mine as a thank you."

Randall chuckled, hooking a finger under the collar to see how tight it was. "A diamond-studded dog collar for a man. Now I've seen everything."

Max gave Hannah a squeeze, then waved to someone behind them. "There's Christian." The man Penelope had seen making out with Hannah in the bathroom approached the bar. He had changed into jeans and a blue dress shirt unbuttoned to his belt. Penelope wondered if he always wore clothes that showed off his intricate cross tattoo. Max made introductions all around. When Christian went to shake hands with Penelope, she averted her eyes and murmured, "Nice to meet you."

"It's so wonderful to finally meet you all. Max has said such nice things," Christian said. He had the same nervous energy as Max, seeming to vibrate even though he was standing still. Penelope wondered if it was performance nerves or guilt stemming from making out with Max's girlfriend. Penelope watched Hannah silently study her wineglass as he spoke.

Another one of the models from the show made his way over to them, standing behind Christian and waving at the busy bartender. "Hanging at your place again tonight?" he said loudly to Christian.

"Yeah, man. We always do," Christian responded. "Guys, this is Jesse."

"Are we going straight there or hitting another club first?" Max asked, finishing his beer.

"Another club?" Arlena asked.

"We're standing in a club," Randall said, waving at the crowd in the main room. Loud music began playing and several people headed to the dance floor.

"A different club, Dad," Max said. "Christian can get us in anywhere."

Randall laughed and finished his martini. "That's nice, son, but I can get in anywhere I want."

Joey placed his hand on Penelope's back and whispered in her ear, "You wanna get out of here?"

"Yes," Penelope said, kissing him before turning back to her friends. "We're going to head out."

Sienna floated over, dressed in a black pantsuit, long blond hair piled on top of her head in a messy bun.

"I'm so pleased you were all able to make it. Max was a dream to work with," Sienna said graciously, her British accent clipping her words.

"Congratulations on a perfect debut," Arlena said. "I'm so proud of you, Sienna."

"I appreciate that. I do think it came off okay."

One of the butlers sidled up to Sienna and whispered something in her ear. A brief look of alarm crossed her face before she regained her composure. "So sorry, I must run. Yet another crisis. You'll excuse me, won't you? Arlena, I'll be in touch soon about that thing we discussed." Sienna hurried off, the butler ushering her away.

"Are we ready to go?" Max asked.

"Absolutely. Let's go to Hydra," Christian said. "It will be packed, but we won't have to wait in line. They still owe me, so we'll get bottle service."

"Owe you?" Max asked.

"I did some free promo for them to welcome them to the neighborhood, brought some of my best faces."

"You have to call me the next time you're opening a club. I'll be one of your faces," Max said.

"What are you talking about?" Arlena asked.

"Christian is a club promoter. Owners hire him to bring models to openings to create buzz, let people know what the new hot spots are."

"All bought and paid for," Randall said, shaking his head. "Really great places earn their reputations over time."

"They've figured out a faster way to get people in the door. They just follow you around," Arlena said to Christian.

"How do you get hired for something like that?" Max asked.

"The jobs come through my agency, and then I coordinate the models. I end up going out a few times a week. Who's coming?"

"You guys go on ahead," Randall said, glancing over the crowd. Penelope followed his gaze to see if he was eyeing anyone in particular but couldn't tell for sure. "I haven't been here in a while. I'm going to see if my name is still on the wall in the men's room."

"Daddy, please be good," Arlena said.

CHAPTER 5

Penelope's high heels tapped the sidewalk as she and Joey strolled through the streets of lower Manhattan, her head still buzzing from the music at Xapa.

She placed her hand in the crook of Joey's arm as they walked, glancing up occasionally at the apartment buildings when the bluish glow of a television caught her eye.

"You're being quiet," Joey said after they'd walked a few blocks.

Penelope shook her head and squeezed his arm. "Sorry, I don't mean to be. I saw something back at the club, but I'm not sure if I really saw what I think I saw. I don't know."

"Anything I can help with?" Joey asked, a note of concern entering his voice.

"No, it's not important. It's not even any of my business."

"That's cryptic," Joey said, smiling at her as they paused at a crosswalk, waiting for the light to turn.

Penelope sighed. "Sorry, it's just, I saw Max's girlfriend making out with that other model Christian when I went to the bathroom."

"So?" Joey asked.

"Right. It's nothing. Forget it." She looked up at the street sign and saw they were standing on the corner of Mulberry and Broome.

"Is he serious about this girl, to the point you feel obligated to say something to him about what you saw?" Joey asked.

"No," Penelope said quickly. "When you put it that way, it

sounds ridiculous. I shouldn't interfere." Penelope regretted bringing it up in the first place, and quickly changed the subject. "Where are we headed, Detective?"

Joey relented, his arm relaxing under her touch. "It's a surprise."

When they turned the corner onto Mulberry, Italian flags hung from the buildings and the smell of roasted tomatoes permeated the air. They walked past a few butcher shops and delis that were closed for the day but still had lengths of salami hanging in the windows.

"Wow, Little Italy," Penelope said. "I haven't been down here in years."

"It's not what it used to be, but there are still a few good spots. You hungry? I thought we could get a late supper."

"Definitely," Penelope said as they stopped in front of a small restaurant with a crescent-shaped sign that read *Luna Ristorante*, which, despite the late hour, bustled with diners. The tablecloths were slick red and white checkerboard plastic, and each of them had a large carafe of red wine in the center next to bottles of olive oil.

They were led to a table in the center of the room with two bright blue ladder-backed chairs. As Joey took the seat opposite Penelope and settled in, their waiter said, "Welcome to Luna. Please, have some wine," he motioned to the carafe on the table, "and take your time to decide what you'd like." He pointed at a large chalkboard on the wall. Several options were available for the evening, ranging from simple spaghetti to eggplant parmesan and Italian seafood stew. After a quick bow he backed away from the table, being careful not to bump the patrons who sat right next to them.

"They don't use printed menus here because it's different every day," Joey said, squinting at the wall.

Joey poured them each some wine. When the waiter returned after a few minutes they made their dinner orders, seafood stew for Joey and *Bronzino Livarnese* for Penelope.

"How did you find this place?" Penelope asked, after the waiter had stepped away.

"I've been coming here since we were kids," Joey said, tearing into a garlic knot from the bowl on the table. "My parents love this place. Nine times out of ten when they come into the city, they stop at Luna for dinner."

"How are your parents doing?" Penelope asked.

"Good. Still in the same house in Jersey," Joey said. He took a quick sip of wine. "Actually, I was wondering..." He trailed off, his cheeks reddening under his dark stubble.

"What?" Penelope said, placing a hand over his.

"Maybe you don't want to, but I was wondering if you'd like to come over one weekend so they could say hello." He picked up the bottle of wine and busied himself with refilling their tumblers.

"Yes, of course. I'd love to see them again."

Joey relaxed a bit. "They remember you from back when we were kids, and I mentioned we were friends again. They said you should come by for dinner one night."

Penelope's heart sank but she managed a smile. "That would be nice. Your parents were always so nice to all the kids on the block."

"Ma loves kids. She's still sad that we all grew up and moved away."

Penelope took a sip of wine and thought about what to say next. She mulled over Joey's comment about them being "friends," when she considered them much more than that. Before she could think of anything to say, their waiter reappeared and placed their dinners down in front of them.

Joey rubbed his palms together. "You have to try some of this stew. It has to cool down a minute though."

Penelope took a bite of her fish, which tasted amazing and was perfectly cooked. "How do you want to get back to Jersey? Do you want to take a train or try and make the last ferry to Hoboken?"

Joey picked up his spoon and stirred his stew a bit, releasing steam into the air. "I have another surprise for you, Penny Blue."

Penelope's fork paused on its way to her mouth. "What's that?"

Joey's cheeks reddened once again, either from embarrassment or from the Chianti. "I booked us a room at Tribeca Loft. I thought we could spend some time in the city, maybe take a walk in the park or hit a museum tomorrow. That's why I didn't ride in with you guys. I packed some of our things and dropped them off before I got to the club."

Penelope took the bite of her fish and swallowed. "The Tribeca Loft? That's pretty fancy. Do you take all of your friends there?"

Joey looked at her, his expression morphing from hopeful expectation to confusion and finally understanding. He chuckled and said in a low voice, "Penny, you know how I feel about you. I told my ma we're friends because you can't imagine the interrogation I'd have to go through if I told her we were dating. I'm not ready for that horror show."

Penelope took another bite and leveled her gaze, chewing slowly, not responding.

Joey looked around them nervously, hoping none of their fellow diners were picking up on their conversation. "Penny, come on. Italian mothers and their sons? You don't even wanna know." He shifted in his chair and picked up the carafe of wine again, his shoulders sagging when he saw it was almost empty.

As if on cue the waiter approached with a replacement carafe, swiftly setting it down and swapping out the empty one without saying a word.

Penelope continued to stare at Joey, betraying no emotion on her face.

"I know it must sound like I don't want to tell them about you. Which is true, but not for the reason you're probably thinking. My kid brother brought a girl home who wasn't from the neighborhood and they acted as if the world was ending. I don't want them to make you feel bad, because I really care about you, Penny Blue." A pleading note had entered his voice.

Penelope relented a bit and put down her fork, folding her hands in her lap. She chewed the inside of her cheek for a few seconds before saying, "I am from the neighborhood, remember? At least I used to be."

Joey sighed, relieved she was talking again. "Yes, that's true. You're not Italian though."

Penelope rolled her eyes. "Really? Joey, it's not 1950. Do you honestly think your parents are going to disapprove of me because I'm not Italian?"

Joey laughed nervously and glanced around them again. "This restaurant has been here since before they were born and this is their regular joint. My parents are really old school, Penny. But you're right. I should be honest and tell them about us. So pick a day and we'll go for dinner." He picked up his spoon and, with a sense of finality, took a bite of stew.

Penelope watched him chew for a bit. After a full minute of silence she said, "How do you feel about me, Joey?"

"Hmm?" Joey said looking up from his bowl, his mouth full.

"You said 'you know how I feel about you,' but I want to hear you tell me how you feel about me in your own words." Penelope braced herself for his answer, hoping she wasn't going to be very disappointed in the next minute.

Joey appeared to search for something on the tablecloth in front of him before raising his eyes to hers. "Obviously, I'm in love with you."

Penelope's heart did a quick series of beats and she took a deep, silent breath. "Good. I feel the same way."

CHAPTER 6

The buzzing inside Penelope's head kept getting louder as she tried to find the restrooms at the end of the dark hallway inside Xapa. This time there were multiple doors on either side, and the hallway was endless, falling off into blackness beyond where she could see. She knew Joey was behind one of the doors, but she couldn't remember how to find him. She stopped at one on the right and pushed. It swung open and she fell forward into the room, the earth dropping away below her feet. She fell through the floor, which had somehow turned to liquid, into a hidden room below. Her parents were waiting for her at their old dining room table, and sitting across from them were Joey's parents. They were all still young and pretending to eat invisible food from empty plates.

Penelope sat straight up in bed in the hotel room. She cleared her throat and looked around, raising a hand to her forehead to fend off the hammer that had started pounding there. An ice bucket holding an empty champagne bottle sweated on the table next to two half-filled flutes. Looking through the gap in the curtains she could tell it was still dark outside. Joey was lying next to her on his stomach, snoring quietly.

Penelope stumbled out of bed towards the ornately carved wall unit and mini refrigerator. She drank most of a bottle of water, swaying on her feet, her long t-shirt brushing her legs just above the knees.

She heard the buzzing sound again from her dream, but this

time recognized it as her phone ringing. She retrieved her phone from one of the club chairs and glanced at the screen. She saw she had a missed call from Max and a three-minute voicemail, time-stamped at three fifteen in the morning.

"What the heck, Max?" Penelope whispered. She tapped the screen to listen to the voicemail, pulling aside the heavy curtain to glance down at the street, the asphalt slick with rain. A single yellow cab bounced slowly down the avenue, its for-hire lamp blurred by the raindrops on the hotel window.

Penelope closed her eyes and shook her head as she realized Max must have called her accidentally. The voicemail was just background noises and thumping sounds, like the phone was in his pocket. "I can't believe Max butt-dialed me at three in the morning," Penelope murmured. She turned her attention back to the voicemail when she heard a woman with a British accent talking and laughing in the background, then what sounded like a door slamming. Penelope rolled her eyes and thought about Hannah, Max's cute little girlfriend from his reality show. She had already decided what Hannah did with Christian, or with Max, or with both of them, was none of her business. The dating world had changed dramatically in the short amount of time since Penelope had been their age. Maybe everyone really did date in groups now. She glanced at Joey sleeping soundly on the bed, the white bedsheets twisted around his calves.

A man's voice suddenly cursed loudly, cutting through the fog in Penelope's brain. She almost dropped the phone but recovered quickly and pressed it tightly to her ear, listening intently to the sounds of a struggle on the other end. She heard someone shout, "You can't do this!" and then more tussling on the other end of the line. Another man shouted, "Shut up or I'll kill you!" and then the message cut off. Penelope pulled the phone away from her ear. She stared at the screen, silent and glowing in the dark. She looked again at Joey, her heart thudding in her chest. She played the message again, shifting her weight from foot to foot and listening more closely to the background noises in the beginning of the message. She couldn't make out what they were talking about. She could only clearly hear them when they were shouting.

She sat down on the club chair near the window and licked her lips, her finger hovering over the call back button. If Max was in some kind of trouble, she definitely wanted to help him. But she didn't want to get involved in a lovers' quarrel or get in the middle of whatever he had going on with Hannah and Christian.

Penelope decided to call and make sure Max was okay. She dialed and gingerly held the phone to her ear, counting the rings. She was about to hang up when someone answered, fumbling with the phone and then dropping it on the other end.

"Hello?" Penelope said. "Max? Are you okay?"

She could hear someone pick up the phone.

"Max! Are you there?" Penelope said, raising her voice. Joey mumbled something in his sleep and rolled onto his side.

"Penelope," Max mumbled into the phone. "Help."

"What's going on? Where are you?"

"He might be dead," Max slurred thickly. "Shot."

"Who's dead? Max!" Penelope shouted.

Joey sat up in bed, his expression a mix of alarm and confusion. "Penny, what's going on?" He reached over and switched on the bedside lamp. Penelope raised her hand to quiet him while she tried to hear what Max was saying.

"Christian and Hannah..." Max trailed off, his voice growing heavy and deep, like he was falling asleep.

"Max, where are you?" Penelope said again, her voice loud and calm.

"Christian's, at the agency." Penelope could barely make out what he was saying. She heard footsteps approaching on the other end of the line and then the sound of glass cracking, then dead air.

"Max!" Penelope shouted to no one. She hit redial but her call went straight to voicemail.

Joey pulled the sheets aside and went to her, hugging his arm around her shoulders. "Calm down and tell me everything."

CHAPTER 7

"He said he was at Christian's," Penelope said. She stared at her phone, willing it to give her more information. "Over the agency. I have no idea what that means."

Joey hugged her again and kissed the top of her head. "What else did you hear?"

"I don't know. I think he called me by mistake, and then I heard an argument on my voicemail." Penelope played the message for Joey, putting her phone on speaker. "I called him back, and when he picked up he sounded scared. He was whispering like maybe he was hiding. And then he said someone was dead. I think someone walked over and smashed his phone after that."

"We're going to figure out what happened," Joey soothed. "Who is this Christian? The guy from the club?"

"Yes, the one with the cross tattoo. We talked to him at the bar before we left."

"Okay, we just have to figure out where he lives."

"I don't know his last name," Penelope said. She glanced at the time on the screen of her phone. Only ten minutes had passed. "It's the middle of the night, but maybe I should call Arlena."

"She's not going to know the guy's name. There's no point in upsetting her before we have more information. Hannah or Sienna would know," Joey said.

"I think Hannah was with them," Penelope said. "Maybe Max was talking about Christian's modeling agency. If Sienna hired him through there she'd know which one he's with."

"Good call," Joey said. He looked around the room, then got up to retrieve his pants from the floor. "Call Xapa. Bars in the city are open 'til four. Maybe Sienna is still there."

She looked up the number for Xapa on her phone. "It's ringing," she said to Joey. She looked again into the night sky through the falling raindrops. It was coming down faster now and a distant streak of lightning smudged the purple sky.

"Xapa," a male voice answered after several rings. His voice was muffled and loud music pounded in the background.

"Hi. Is Sienna Wentworth still there? The fashion designer? We were at her show earlier."

"I don't know," the man said. "I think they packed up their stuff and left a while ago." He yelled indistinctly to someone away from the phone. "Hang on a second."

Penelope eased herself down, perching on the edge of the chair, and watched Joey go into the bathroom. He turned on the light and squinted into the mirror.

Penelope listened to the music over the phone, pressing the phone tightly to her ear. After a few minutes the man came back on the line. "Most everyone is gone, but I found one of the models from the show. You want to talk to him?"

"Yes, please," Penelope said. She heard the phone fumbling between hands and muffled voices.

"Hello?" a man's quiet voice said.

"Hi, I'm Penelope Sutherland, a friend of Sienna's. Do you know where she is?"

"No, she left a while ago. I don't know where they went."

"Maybe you know one of the other models, the one who came out at the end, with the tattoos? His name is Christian." Penelope watched Joey pull a clean t-shirt from his overnight bag.

"Christian." He said the name in a Spanish-sounding accent. "Yeah, I know him. He left a long time ago too." His words slurred together, most likely from a long night drinking at Xapa.

"Do know where he lives?" Penelope asked.

"He lives in Chelsea above his modeling agency, off of Seventh

Avenue," he said. Penelope could hear ice clinking in his glass on the other end of the phone.

"Do you know which agency he's with?" Penelope asked.

"I don't know. Something that starts with an M. Said he has lots of parties. Told the other guys from the show to come over whenever they wanted, he has party favors and pretty girls. And boys. I thought that was weird, like, who invites random strangers over to their house?" The man put his hand over the receiver. Penelope heard him shout to someone over the loud club music.

"Can you remember anything else about the building? I need to find it," Penelope asked, clenching her fist in her lap.

"He said it's an older building close to the avenue, not very tall. He acted like we should all have heard of this agency, but I never have. Honestly, I wasn't really paying attention. I walked away while they were all still talking about it."

Penelope thanked him for his help and hung up. "It might be a modeling agency that starts with the letter M in Chelsea near Seventh."

"That narrows it down. There can't be too many that fit that description," Joey said.

"Right." Penelope Googled modeling agencies in Chelsea and sighed in relief. "Oh good, there's only a page or two of listings."

"Find the ones that start with M and map them."

Penelope scrolled through the results on her screen. "I hope the guy on the phone got the first letter right or we'll never find it. Do you think we should we call the police?"

"Yes," Joey said. "But we should try and find out what happened first, so we know what to tell them."

Penelope nodded and glanced back at her phone. "Here's one. Models Unlimited International, MUI. It's on 20th near Seventh Avenue."

"Call the number, see if anyone picks up," Joey said. He sat down in the other lounge chair and drank the rest of Penelope's water.

Penelope dialed the main number listed for MUI and after a

few rings got the company voicemail, putting the phone on speaker for Joey to hear.

"It was worth a try," Joey said. "I was thinking if it was a privately run agency then maybe it was someone's house. Are you sure about what you heard on the phone when you called Max back? It's late and they must have been partying for hours if they were headed to other clubs. Maybe they're just goofing around."

Penelope paused for a moment, remembering the fear in Max's voice. "He sounded scared. I've never heard him like that. I just get the feeling that something terrible has happened." She looked at Joey with uncertainty.

"Okay, get dressed and let's go to Chelsea," Joey said.

CHAPTER 8

The cab sped north on the West Side Highway, rain tapping on the roof and windows fogging against the damp air. Penelope had thrown on a t-shirt and jeans, and a pair of running shoes Joey had packed in his overnight bag for her before rushing out of their hotel room.

"Arlena must have her phone off. It just goes to voicemail." Penelope ended another unsuccessful call. "I hope she gets my messages."

They didn't have an umbrella or anything else to protect them from the rain, so they'd be soaked the moment they stepped outside. Doubt began to nip at the edges of Penelope's mind and she glanced at Joey, who was staring past the Plexiglas divider and out through the windshield. She hoped her concern for Max was justified and she hadn't pulled them out of their luxury hotel suite into the chilly rain for no reason.

The driver pulled up at the corner and Joey slid his credit card through the fare machine. They stepped out onto Seventh Avenue and looked around, squinting through the raindrops.

"Here, let's go," Joey said, ushering her toward 20th Street. "Look for the address you found."

Penelope tucked her hair behind her ear, already wet from the rain as they hurried along the street, huddling close to each other.

"There it is." Penelope pointed to a small brownstone a few doors down from a shuttered bodega. MUI was printed in gold letters on the glass of the wooden double doors. Penelope bounded up the stoop and looked at the buzzers on the call box. The first three were unlabeled but the fourth had a sticker next to it with an intricate drawing of a cross.

"This is definitely the place," Penelope said, pointing at the drawing that resembled the tattoos on Christian's chest. She reached out to ring the bell and Joey grabbed her wrist.

"Wait a minute," he said. "Let me take a look first." He went back down the steps and squinted at the windows above the stoop while Penelope shivered under the narrow awning over the front door. Joey walked around to the side of the building and glanced through an iron gate that led to a patio area sandwiched between the agency and the neighboring brownstone. After a few minutes Joey returned to the stoop.

"The lights are on up on the top floor apartment, but I didn't see anyone moving around. Go ahead and ring the bell."

Penelope pressed the top buzzer and waited. The intercom clicked twice, but no one answered and the door didn't open. She pressed the buzzer again and looked at Joey.

"Let's go around the side," Joey said. "There's another entrance off the patio...could be the apartment entrance." Penelope was grateful the rain had let up some, but her clothes were still soaked through, her t-shirt sticking to her back.

Joey swung open the gate and it glided easily toward them with a quiet groan of metal on metal. He pulled a thin flashlight from his pants pocket and shined it into the courtyard and up the back of the building. There were unlit twinkly lights strung over the patio and a couple of wrought-iron tables and matching chairs scattered around. Two wooden storm doors that led down to the basement of the brownstone were padlocked, and next to them was a small concrete stoop leading up to the side door. There was a set of buzzers on the wall next to the door, but Penelope knew right away she wouldn't be using them. One of the four glass panes of the window was broken and the door was ajar.

"Oh no," Penelope said when Joey pointed his flashlight down at the steps. There were red smears on the glass and a trail of blood drops leading down the stairs into the courtyard.

"Stand back," Joey said in a forceful yet calm tone. He reached around to the small of his back and pulled a gun from his waistband.

"You have your gun with you?" Penelope whispered, still shocked by the sight of the blood. She was afraid to move from where she was standing for fear of stepping in any of it.

"It's my off-duty weapon. It's always with me," Joey said, keeping his voice low. "Do me a favor, call 911. Hopefully whatever happened here is over," he nodded at the blood drops heading away from the building, disappearing on the rainy pavement of the patio, "but we can't know that for sure. We don't need to be walking in on anything upstairs without backup." He jogged down the steps and trained his flashlight on the ground, darting the beam around as he followed the blood trail out to the sidewalk. He paused for a moment, then walked out of sight, heading left.

Penelope pulled her phone from her jeans pocket and dialed 911. She willed her hands to stop shaking, both from the cold and from the fear she suddenly felt, realizing she was alone on the stoop.

"911, what's your emergency?"

"Yes, I'm calling to report—"

Just then the door banged open and knocked her halfway down the stoop, her phone flying from her hand. It landed on the pavement and skidded all the way to the wall of the neighboring building. She felt someone shove her from behind as she tried to regain her footing on the steps, and she was flying through the air. She instinctively put her arms up to shield her face as she fell, landing awkwardly against one of the tables then bouncing off of it and onto her back underneath it. Dazed, she looked at the door and saw it bouncing on its hinges, and then towards the street where she saw a man running away from her, a duffle bag bouncing off his hip, red running shoes flashing quickly into the darkness.

"Stop! Police!" She heard Joey shouting from the sidewalk.

Penelope caught a glimpse of both of them running to the right toward the avenue. And then she heard a gunshot.

Penelope pulled herself into a ball under the table, closing her eyes and covering her head with her forearms. Her eyes popped open when she heard a police siren, more shouting from the street, and screeching tires.

"I'm on the job," Joey said, his arms raised in the air as he walked back towards the brownstone. Two patrol officers jumped from their vehicle, weapons drawn and pointed at him.

"What's the color of the day?" one of the officers yelled, asking Joey to confirm the daily safe word for officers out of uniform in the city.

"I'm not New York, I don't know. I'm Jersey Homicide, Detective Joseph Baglioni."

Penelope pulled herself up with the help of the patio table and stood shakily next to it.

"Let me see your hands," the female police officer demanded. Penelope raised her hands slowly in the air.

"You have to help us. I think my friend is hurt upstairs," Penelope said.

The officer nearest Joey made his way to him, spun him around, frisked him, and seized his gun. Over his protests, the officer sat Joey in the back of the patrol car, his hands cuffed behind him. The female officer walked through the gate and approached Penelope, her gun drawn.

"You have blood on you," she said, eyeing Penelope up and down.

"Did you see him? Did you see the man with the duffle bag? He had on jeans, I think, and red running shoes. He pushed past me and took off. He came from up there," Penelope said, pointing to the roof of the brownstone with one raised hand.

"Okay, calm down," the officer said, holstering her weapon. "I'm going to search you now, okay? Do you have anything sharp in your pockets, any needles?"

Penelope shook her head no.

"What's your name? You have ID?" She turned Penelope around to face the table and began patting her down from behind.

"I'm Penelope Sutherland. And I don't. My ID is back at the hotel. I just have my phone," Penelope said, glancing into the darkness at where she thought her phone had landed. She finally saw the edge of it at the base of the building, lying upside down in a puddle.

"What are you doing here tonight? A little breaking and entering?" the officer asked, turning Penelope around and patting down her front.

Penelope glanced at the patrol car and saw Joey staring at her through the window in the backseat. The rain started falling again, bouncing off the black plastic rim of the officer's cap.

Penelope shook her head, recovering from the shock of her fall. She took a deep breath. "Please, Officer..." she glanced at the woman's nameplate over her badge, "Gomez. I think my friend might be hurt upstairs. That's why we're here. My boyfriend," she nodded towards the patrol car, "is a police officer. I got a call from my friend earlier. We were here trying to track him down, to make sure he's okay."

Officer Gomez nodded and turned Penelope around towards the building. "We'll see about that."

Penelope looked up at the windows on the fourth floor. She heard the sound of Velcro ripping and the metal clink of handcuffs. Her stomach dropped and her heart started pounding in her chest.

"You guys been doing a little drinking tonight, huh? Thought you'd come around here, quiet neighborhood, and what? Do a little shopping?"

Penelope shook her head, still staring at the windows. "No. I swear, we just came to see about my friend. Can you please see if he's okay?"

"I think you decided to break the window on this house," Officer Gomez said. "And then your man over there takes a shot at someone out on the street? What, did he rip you off or something? You're going to have to do better than this cock and bull story. We get a lot of druggies around here, looking to rip people off. Don't lie to me."

A streak of lightning lit the sky over them and thunder rumbled in the distance. A fresh wave of rain began falling, splashing up from the pavement. Penelope heard Officer Gomez un-cinch the handcuffs and felt her grab her right wrist.

Penelope jerked her hand free, her wet skin slipping through the officer's grasp. Without thinking she bolted up the stoop, pulled open the door, and ran as fast as she could up the wooden staircase inside.

"Hey! Stop!" Officer Gomez yelled behind her. Penelope heard the door bang open again and her heavy boots on the stairs behind her.

Penelope's wet sneakers slipped on the wooden steps and her hand skidded on the railing as she rounded the first three landings. She didn't dare look behind her to see how close Officer Gomez was to her. When she got to the top, she saw that the door to the apartment was open. It was black with a cross etched onto it in chalky white paint. Beyond the door she could see the room was brightly lit and appeared to have been ransacked. Tables were overturned and couch cushions had been sliced through. Penelope pushed the door open all the way and stepped inside. She breathed heavily, her wet hair dripping in ringlets onto the floor around her shoes. Five seconds later, Officer Gomez was next to her. They both stood rigidly in the entryway, staring in silence, trying to catch their breath.

There was a large pool of blood right inside the door that at least one set of shoes had walked through.

"Backup and a bus needed ASAP near the corner of 20th and Seventh, last location patrol three-seven-zero responded to…"

Officer Gomez's voice faded away as Penelope took in the scene in front of her. Blood trailed from the door back into the main room of the loft toward the kitchen. She traced it with her eye and saw that it ended near a man's legs, splayed on the floor, his pants soaked red.

"Oh my God," Penelope said, her knees turning to rubber. She began a shaky walk into the apartment but was stopped abruptly when Officer Gomez grabbed her by the forearm.

"Not a chance," she said harshly. "You're under arrest."

CHAPTER 9

Officer Gomez pulled Penelope back out onto the landing and handcuffed her. "Let's go," she demanded, nodding down the stairway.

"Please," Penelope said through her tears. "I have to see if my friend is in there."

Officer Gomez turned Penelope around roughly and looked closely at her face. She pulled out a penlight and shone it into her eyes. "Open your mouth."

Penelope hesitated a moment then opened wide, showing the woman her teeth.

Officer Gomez eyed her up and down once more. "You don't look like a junkie now that I can see you better." She radioed to her partner downstairs, who confirmed that Joey was on the job. Her tough expression relented and she said, "Tell me again what you think happened here tonight."

Penelope's knees buckled with relief, even though she was still handcuffed and technically under arrest. "I got a weird message from my friend, Max Madison."

"Max Madison. Randall Madison's son? The one from the MTV show?" Officer Gomez asked.

Penelope nodded. "I heard some kind of argument. We tracked down where we thought Max might be and called 911. We were trying to decide what to do next when a man came running out the door and knocked me down. Joey chased him up the block, and I heard a shot. Then you guys showed up. Please, you have to help Max," Penelope begged, looking back at the apartment door.

Officer Gomez shook her head slightly and pressed the radio on her lapel. "Has our backup arrived?"

"Copy, they're on their way up to you now," her partner responded. They heard the door open below them and both glanced towards the stairway. "The boss is on his way too. We're detaining Detective Baglioni for discharging his weapon."

Officer Gomez nodded. "Copy." She turned to Penelope. "Stay right here. Don't make me chase you again."

Penelope nodded quickly. "Thank you, I will."

Two uniformed officers joined them on the landing. "Follow me. The scene isn't cleared yet, so stay alert. Let's check in all the usual hiding places." The three of them pulled their weapons and entered the apartment.

Penelope pushed the small of her back against the wooden railing on the landing and listened to them move through the apartment. They didn't say much during their search, until she heard three voices say "Clear."

"I've got one male DOA, gunshot wounds to the chest and abdomen. Clear signs of a struggle, possibly additional victims, multiple blood trails. We'll need detectives and CSU up here," Officer Gomez said into her radio.

Penelope felt sick to her stomach as she watched the two officers walk past her and down the stairs. Officer Gomez came out of the door and faced her. "It's not Max. It's a big guy. Blond."

"The guy who lives here is named Christian. He's got a bunch of cross tattoos," Penelope said.

"Then that's probably him," Officer Gomez said, glancing quickly at the legs sticking out from the alcove. "He your friend too?" When Penelope shook her head she said, "Turn around."

Officer Gomez undid the handcuffs and Penelope rubbed the red marks on her wrists where they had pinched the skin. "Let's go back downstairs," Officer Gomez said. A drop of kindness had slipped into her voice.

When they walked back outside, the rain had stopped. Joey was on the sidewalk next to the patrol car he'd been sitting in, talking to a man in a white uniform shirt with several ribbons pinned over his badge. Two more patrol cars were parked behind the first one and an ambulance slid up silently behind them, red lights bouncing off of the surrounding buildings. Penelope noticed a few curtains had been pulled aside across the street by curious neighbors who'd had their sleep disrupted. She glanced up at the windows of the brownstone that shared the courtyard with Christian's building and saw a woman gazing down from the third floor window, pulling apart her wooden blinds to see what all the commotion was about.

Penelope hurried over to Joey. When he saw her approaching, he nodded quickly at the police captain he'd been talking to and rushed over to meet her, grabbing her up in his arms and hugging her.

"Ouch," Penelope said, feeling for the first time pain in her ribs from falling against the table.

"Sorry. Penny, please don't do that again. You had me worried sick," he said, burying his face in her hair. He held her for a moment longer. "I have to go in with them, do some paperwork."

"She's coming in too," Officer Gomez said, walking up behind them. "We're going to need statements from you both."

CHAPTER 10

Penelope sat in a lumpy guest chair next to a cluttered metal desk in the center of the lower Manhattan squad room. She looked through the glass window of the captain's office and watched the back of Joey's head as he spoke to the stern-faced man, his white hair perfectly matching his shirt. He frowned as he listened to Joey, switching between leaning forward on his desk with his fingers tightly entwined and leaning back in his chair with his arms crossed at his chest. She glanced down at her shattered phone and ran her finger along the cracks in the glass.

"Please review the statement as given and sign here, ma'am." A pudgy detective returned to the desk where she sat and handed her a folder with three yellow-lined typed sheets attached by metal clips. She read through the statement and signed it at the bottom of the last page. The detective took the folder from her and tossed it onto a teetering stack of papers on his desk. A chipped nameplate next to it read Det. John Leary.

"What are the next steps to finding Max?"

Detective Leary eyed her with tired irritation. "Ma'am, as I explained to you before, I have no idea if your friend is missing, fled the scene of a crime, or is just sleeping it off somewhere. It's too early to tell what happened in that apartment. One thing I know for sure is I got a dead body, and that's my priority right now."

Penelope looked back down at her phone, exhaustion pulling her shoulders down.

"Look," the detective said with a note of kindness, "I know you're worried about your friend, but people have a way of turning up. From what you told me, a bunch of people were out, drinking at lots of different places...any number of things could have happened. He's probably asleep on a couch somewhere right now. You can't even tell me for sure if he was in that building."

Penelope looked up at him. "Yeah, but on the message—"

"The message that no longer exists," the detective said, glancing at her cracked phone. "Even if you could get the message, what would I be able to hear? A fight? Without a location or a body..."

Penelope sucked in a gasp and tears pricked the corners of her eyes.

Detective Leary sighed. "Sorry. Look, I've been doing this a long time. He's going to turn up and probably have quite a story to tell. My advice to you is go home and wait for him. And get some rest."

Penelope regained her composure and stared blankly at him.

"We'll be in touch if we have any questions. You're free to go."

Penelope looked back at the window and saw Joey leaving the captain's office, angrily yanking open the door as he went. She jumped up from her seat and hurried over to him.

"You finished here?" he asked when he saw her approaching.

"Yes, they just said I could go," Penelope said.

"Good," Joey said tightly, ushering her towards the exit door of the squad room.

"Is everything okay?" Penelope asked.

"Not here," Joey said, hurrying her along.

When they stepped outside it was morning, the sun rising brightly over the East River. A group of police officers stood near the front steps, and Penelope saw Officer Gomez with them. She had changed out of her uniform into street clothes, jeans and a pink long-sleeved t-shirt, her hair hanging in loose curls down her back. Her large gold hoop earrings caught the glint of the sun as she turned to look at Penelope.

"One minute, Joey," Penelope said, walking over to her.

"Rough night, eh?" Officer Gomez asked as Penelope approached. "You look like you could use some sleep."

Penelope nodded. "Can I ask you something?"

"Okay," Officer Gomez said apprehensively.

"I don't think the detective I spoke to in there is going to look for Max," Penelope said.

Officer Gomez glanced back at the group of officers talking with each other near the entrance and took Penelope's arm, moving her away from them. She flicked a strand of black hair over her shoulder. "Look, we only have your word that anything even happened to him. A cell phone call can be made from anywhere. He's not a missing person. Right now there's no evidence he was involved."

"We helped you find Christian, doesn't that count for anything? I'm not making this up," Penelope said.

"I know you think he's in trouble, I get that." Officer Gomez glanced over her shoulder again at her colleagues and lowered her voice. "Here's some free advice. I wouldn't be trying so hard to link Max with Christian if I were you. Why do you think we were on you so fast?"

"Because I called 911?" Penelope said.

Officer Gomez laughed and shook her head. "We get called to that location all the time. We were responding to a complaint from a neighbor before your call even came through. So unless you want your friend to be caught up in a criminal investigation, I'd keep your theories to yourself. You get me?"

Penelope bit her bottom lip and looked over at Joey. His arms were crossed and he had his back to them. "Is there anything else you can do?"

"Who, me?" Officer Gomez said with a look of surprise. "I did do something. I believed you were telling the truth and I didn't arrest you, even though I had more than enough to bring you in." She started ticking off her fingers. "Trespassing, resisting arrest, breaking and entering, assaulting an officer..."

"Assaulting? Come on," Penelope said, taking a step away from her. "I was just trying to find out what happened to Max."

"And now you have to leave it to the police. If he was there and there is evidence that he was involved with drugs or anything else illegal in that apartment, we'll be the ones pursuing him. Don't let me find you in the middle of this again, or I *will* bring you in."

Penelope stared at her for a moment. "Can you at least tell me if they do find anything out about Max?"

Officer Gomez sighed, putting a hand on her hip. She shook her head and pulled a leather business card case from her back pocket. "Here's my card. You can call me if you want. I'll let you know what I can. But remember what I told you. Don't get in the way."

Penelope took the card from her and ran her fingers over the upraised letters of her name: Denise Gomez. "Thanks."

Officer Gomez sniffed and shook her head as she watched Penelope walk away.

CHAPTER 11

Penelope and Joey rode in the back of the cab in silence, Joey staring out the window at the Hudson River as they traveled down the West Side Highway.

"Are you okay?" Penelope asked, looking at the back of his head.

Joey sighed and remained silent, both of them rocking on the seat when the cab braked suddenly for slow traffic.

"Joey, what happened?" Penelope asked quietly.

"I winged the guy," Joey said. "I know I hit him in the arm, but he kept running. I didn't want to get too far away from you in case anyone else came out. We never should have gone over there in the first place. It was stupid of me and now..." He shook his head.

"Now what?" Penelope asked.

"Now I'm on administrative leave until they can clear the shooting. I have to answer not only to my boss but the Manhattan borough chief and explain to them why I discharged my weapon on a residential street while off duty. Not to mention after a night of drinking. I'll be lucky if I just get suspended after everyone is through with me." Joey crossed his arms tightly and stared out through the windshield, willing the traffic to move again.

"Joey, I'm so sorry," Penelope said.

Joey shook his head. "I was worried about you, Penny, about leaving you behind. I'd never forgive myself if anything happened to you. If I had caught the guy, if I'd apprehended him and proven he'd been the one up in Christian's apartment, things would be a lot better. But right now, they just have my word and not much else to go on."

Penelope stared down at her hands as she twisted them in her lap.

Joey rapped his knuckles on the Plexiglas divider to get the cab driver's attention. "Hey, you mind getting off this?"

The cab driver nodded and inched into the left lane so he could take the next exit.

"Joey, I'm sorry I got you involved," Penelope said. "I can't believe it got to be such a mess."

After another minute, the cab freed itself from the gridlock on the highway and began moving quickly again along the bumpy streets of lower Manhattan.

"Look, I know we've got something here, you and me. But Max and Arlena, they're a big part of your life too. I want to be sure I'll be a priority to you if we're going to move forward."

"Of course you are—" Penelope protested.

"Except," Joey cut her off, raising a finger in the air, "when you get a call from Max in the middle of the night, you jump out of bed and run to him. And dummy that I am, I follow right behind you."

"Don't say that," Penelope said quietly, flicking her eyes at the back of the cab driver's head. Joey had turned away from her again. "I'm worried about Max, that's all. If you could've heard how scared he sounded on the phone...I would try and help any of my friends in the same situation."

The tension in Joey's shoulders relented slightly, but his anger was still putting a wall between them. Without looking at her he said, "I'm going to get my things from the room and head back to Jersey. I have to be in my boss's office at noon to answer for all of this. You should stay, get some sleep."

Penelope reached up to place a hand on his shoulder and felt it stiffen beneath her touch.

The cab stopped abruptly in front of the Tribeca Loft, and Joey and Penelope rode the elevator up to their room in silence. Once they were inside, Joey closed the bathroom door behind him and turned on the shower.

Penelope picked up the phone on the bedside table and connected with room service, ordering breakfast for two and a pot of coffee. After she hung up, she laid down on the bed to rest her eyes.

A loud knock on the door woke her and Penelope sat up on the bed, momentarily disoriented. She opened the door to a smiling room service waiter, his hands resting on a rolling cart topped with two silver cloches.

"Breakfast, madam?" he said, smiling brightly.

Penelope rubbed her eyes. "Yes, please come in."

He rolled the cart into the room and busied himself arranging the cloches on the table in front of the windows, setting out the coffee carafe and cups and placing the silverware down with a slight flourish. Penelope glanced at the bathroom and saw the door was open and the lights were off.

"Joey?" Penelope asked, glancing around the room.

The waiter finished setting the table and then looked at her expectantly, his hands tucked neatly behind his back.

Penelope grabbed her handbag from the lounge chair and pulled a ten-dollar bill from it. "Here you go."

"Thank you, madam. Enjoy," he said, bowing quickly and leaving her alone in the room.

Penelope looked around her and saw a stack of her clothes had been neatly folded in a pile on the opposite chair. And Joey's overnight bag was gone.

CHAPTER 12

Penelope sat cross legged in one of the club chairs, slowly chewing a piece of bacon and staring out of the hotel window. She thought about the night before and how everything seemed to go from wonderful to so very wrong in such a short amount of time. She and Joey had taken a big step forward in their relationship during dinner at Luna, and then it felt like they took ten steps back in the cab this morning. This was their first fight, and it felt overwhelming when she thought about Max being in trouble too.

Maybe the detective and Officer Gomez were right and she had misinterpreted the message from Max on her phone. But there was no mistaking the panic she heard in Max's voice when she talked to him. She had no idea how to feel or what to do next. Penelope took a sip of lukewarm coffee from the dainty coffee cup and set it back down on its matching saucer, staring at the words *Tribeca Loft* etched in gold on the inner rim. She went to the bedside phone and called the front desk.

"Good morning, how may I help you?" a young woman's chipper voice answered.

"Hi, I was just wondering what time checkout is."

"Our standard checkout time is one o'clock. Will you be extending your stay past tomorrow?" Penelope could hear her tapping a keyboard over the phone.

"Tomorrow? We have the room for more than one night?" Penelope asked, twisting the phone cord in her fingers.

"Yes, your room is reserved through tonight with a checkout scheduled for Monday at one o'clock. Also, I have a note here from the concierge that your dinner reservations are confirmed for La Modern, and you can pick up your tickets for the show after two this afternoon at the desk."

"Okay," Penelope said, more confused than ever.

"May I assist you with anything else?"

"No," Penelope said, trying to think. "Wait, yes, can you tell me where the nearest Manhattan Cellular is? I have to replace my phone."

"There are two right near here," the woman said, quickly rattling off the addresses. "If you need a map of the city or transit information please stop by the front desk."

Penelope hung up and sat down on the edge of the bed, feeling even worse about everything that happened. Joey had planned a romantic weekend in the city for them, complete with dinner and a show, and now it had blown up in spectacular fashion.

After taking a hot shower and putting on clean clothes, Penelope felt better, at least physically. When she stepped out the front doors of the hotel, she breathed in the morning air which still smelled fresh from the previous night's rain, and walked in the direction of the nearest phone store. Half an hour later, new phone in hand, she stepped back onto the sidewalk and called Max. The call went straight to voicemail. Penelope sighed. "Max, please call me or Arlena right away. I'm worried about you."

Penelope hung up and stuck the phone in her back pocket before ducking into a busy French patisserie for a cup of coffee. She wanted to sit and think about her next move and craved more caffeine. As she stood in line, her phone buzzed and she pulled it out of her back pocket quickly, hoping to see Max's name there. Instead it was Arlena's picture smiling up at her.

"Hi, Arlena," Penelope said.

"Penelope! There you are. I've been trying to call," Arlena said, a note of alarm in her voice.

Penelope stepped out of the coffee line and walked to the front window of the patisserie. "My phone broke last night. I just picked up a new one."

"I got your messages when I woke up. I couldn't understand what you were talking about, just that you were worried about Max. What's going on?" Penelope could hear Sam's voice in the background but couldn't make out what he was saying.

"I was worried about Max because I got this strange message from him. It sounded like he was in trouble, so I went out to try and find him."

"Pen, you know how Max is. I'm sure it was nothing. He drunk-dials me all the time. I've learned to turn my phone off when I know he's going to be out clubbing."

Penelope closed her eyes and perched on one of the tall stools lining the front window, leaning her elbows on the narrow wooden counter. "It's not nothing this time. Arlena, the police found Christian dead in his apartment last night."

"What happened?" Arlena demanded.

Penelope told her everything she could about the night before, starting with the call from Max and ending with the police finding Christian's body. She kept the part about all of the blood in the apartment to herself, thinking that it wouldn't do any good to send Arlena into a panic.

"And we don't know where Max is," Arlena said. She pulled the phone away from her ear. Penelope could hear her relating the news to Sam. There was a moment of silence and then she said, "What did the detective say when he heard the message from Max?"

"He never heard it. My phone broke when we were at Christian's apartment and the message was lost. He only has my word that Max is in trouble, and I don't think he's taking it very seriously," Penelope said.

"Fine. We'll find him ourselves. I'll get in touch with Daddy. He'll know what to do. He didn't come home last night, not that I was expecting him to."

"I'll try and track Max down from here, check for him at his apartment. Where is it again?"

Arlena gave her an address in the West Village.

"Did you guys go with Max to that club Christian was talking about? Hydra?" Penelope asked.

"No, we gave them a ride in the limo and dropped them off. I don't know, one look at the line outside the door...it didn't seem like our kind of crowd. I hate to sound old, but everyone looked like they were sixteen. Sam and I just came home and went to bed. He's got a flight this afternoon."

"So you took Christian, Max, and Hannah in the limo?"

"Yes, they were very happy and excited to be going out. I'm pretty sure they went right up to the door and went in, skipped the line."

"And you didn't hear from Max at all after that?"

"I turned my phone off before we went to bed," Arlena said, regretfully. "But there weren't any messages from him when I woke up. Just from you."

"He called me around three in the morning," Penelope said, "and the police discovered Christian's body, because of us, around four. So we have to try and trace his steps around that time. If I don't find him at his apartment, I can try Hannah's place. Do you have her number?"

"No, I barely know the girl," Arlena said. "But I know the whole cast from Max's show lives together in his building. Maybe they just went home and you'll find them there. Or at least someone who knows where they might be."

"Good idea," Penelope said.

"Okay, you and Joey see what you can find out on your end. I'll find Daddy and keep trying Max's phone. If I get him to answer, I'll call you right away."

"Sounds good," Penelope said. "But it's just me. Joey had to head back to Jersey for a work thing. He may have gotten into trouble last night when we went out to look for Max."

"Oh no," Arlena said. "Are you okay?"

"I'll feel much better when we find Max and make sure he's all right."

Penelope ended the call with Arlena and swiped her screen until she found Joey's number. After two rings her call abruptly flipped into his voicemail, letting her know he'd declined her call.

CHAPTER 13

Penelope trotted down the steps to the subway station, to-go coffee cup in hand. She heard the train entering the station just as she swiped her MetroCard and ran down to the platform, slipping between the doors of the northbound train right before they closed. The subway lurched forward and Penelope grabbed the grimy silver pole to keep herself from falling. The train was about half full, most of the riders staring at their phones or pretending to sleep as they gained speed and dove into the blackness of the tunnel.

Ten minutes later the train pulled into the Christopher Street station and Penelope stepped quickly through the doors, pushed through the turnstile, and jogged up the concrete steps to the sidewalk. She glanced around for a few seconds to orient herself, then headed west towards Bleecker. The building Max lived in was leased by the production company that filmed Max's reality show, and it was in Max's contract that they would provide his housing as long as he remained on the show. The ratings were good and they'd just been picked up for another season, so Penelope figured Max would have a free apartment in the city for at least another year.

Penelope tossed her empty coffee cup in the trash can on the corner of 11th and Bleecker and looked up at the red brick building on the corner. The first floor housed a bookstore, which wasn't yet open for the day. To the left of the store's display window was a black metal doorway with an antique lantern hanging above it and an unmarked brass buzzer panel next to the door. Penelope saw a red indicator light hidden in the entryway, what she assumed was a camera, tiny and round, tucked up in the corner. There was no indication from the outside that this was where the sons and daughters of various celebrities shared a home and filmed a popular reality show.

Penelope pressed the bottom button, hearing a faint buzz past the door in the lobby. She waited a few seconds with no response then pressed the buzzer again. A faint click and pop came through the speaker and a deep male voice said, "Can I help you?"

Penelope pressed the button again. "I'm here to see Max Madison. I'm a friend of his." She glanced up at the camera, assuming the man on the other end would be able to see her face.

"One moment, please," he said.

Penelope took a step back and peered through the window of the door into the white marble foyer. She was just able to see the outer edge of a small reception desk. A short, square-shaped man appeared from behind it and made his way toward her, opening the door and leaning out to speak with her. He had on a dark blue blazer that strained against his thick shoulders and a clear plastic earpiece attached to a tiny spiral cord that disappeared under his collar.

"Hi," Penelope said. "Is Max here?"

The large man looked her up and down, his green eyes set wide apart on his face. "What's your name?"

"Penelope Sutherland. I'm a close friend of the family. We haven't been able to get in touch with Max since last night and we're a little worried about him. Have you seen him this morning?"

The man glanced behind her as someone blared their horn on the street and then back down at Penelope. "Come in," he said, ushering her into the lobby and pulling the door closed behind them. He motioned her over to the reception desk and stepped back behind it, taking his seat and tapping on a computer keyboard. "Okay, Penelope Sutherland..." He squinted at his computer monitor. "Yep, you're on the list of known contacts for Mr. Max."

"Known contacts?" Penelope asked.

"Residents provide us a list of family and friends who they

allow access to the building. They're allowed five names, and your name checks out. Can I see your ID?" he asked with a small smile.

Penelope dug in her handbag and pulled out her license. The security guard glanced at it and nodded.

"Now let's see, Mr. Max..." He tapped his keyboard again. "I do not have him logged in this morning. He left yesterday afternoon around three, but he has not returned according to our records." He leaned back in his armless rolling chair, which groaned in protest against his weight.

"He has to check in and out with you?" Penelope asked.

"No," the man said, still smiling and shaking his head. "They're free to come and go, they don't have to sign out. The security team just makes a notation when the actors pass through the lobby. All guests of the residents have to sign in, of course."

"Do they have a curfew?" Penelope asked, a bit confused by the security procedures. It sounded less like a luxury building and more like a penitentiary.

"No, ma'am. We ~~keep~~ just keep track of them as a safety precaution. The company asks us to." His voice took on a placating tone. "Some of our tenants are young, on their own for the first time in the city. Their parents and the producers like us to keep an eye on them, discreetly, know their whereabouts. They're like employees, insured by the producers."

Penelope pushed her judgmental feelings aside for the moment. "Can you do me a favor and check if Hannah Devore came home last night?"

The man shook his head. "It's okay for me to check on Max for you since he gave his permission for the people on his list. But I have to protect Miss Devore's privacy."

"Oh, okay," Penelope said, unable to hide her disappointment. She also thought for a company that was acting like Big Brother in these young people's lives, it was ironic he was being so secretive now.

"I will tell you," the man said, lowering his voice, "those two do spend a good amount of time together."

Penelope looked at him hopefully. "She's probably not here either, then?"

The man smiled at her and splayed his fingers in a "who knows" gesture.

"Can I take a look at Max's apartment?" Penelope asked.

The man hesitated a moment and narrowed his eyes at Penelope.

"I wouldn't ask, but it's an emergency. There was an incident last night and Max might be in danger."

Concern clouded his features. "You're on Max's list, and he's given everyone on it permission to enter. Take the elevator up to the third floor. He's in 3C. You have a key?"

When Penelope shook her head, he pulled open a drawer below his desk and opened a lockbox, taking a key from it and handing it to her.

"I really appreciate your help," Penelope said.

"You're welcome. Just sign the logbook before you go," he said, flipping open a leather-bound binder on the countertop. Penelope signed in and went to the elevator, throwing a grateful smile at him over her shoulder as the doors slid open.

Max's apartment was at the end of the hall on the third floor. Penelope turned the key in the lock and the door glided open silently on its hinges.

"Max?" Penelope called from the doorway.

Penelope stepped inside the main living area and saw three of Randall's movie posters framed behind the overstuffed black leather couch. The dark wood coffee table was covered with magazines, books, and remote controls and sat low over a white faux-fur throw rug. Penelope sorted through the magazines, most of them about entertainment or men's health. He had quite a collection of tabloids and he was reading a couple of different books. A paperback mystery lay open upside down on the coffee table and a bookmark was stuck in the middle of a large book titled *The Tragedies: Sixteen Greek Plays*.

Penelope went to Max's small kitchen and opened the

refrigerator. There were various takeout containers inside and a bottle of white wine chilling on the door, but not much else. She glanced into the trash bin and saw it was lined with a clean white bag, with just a few discarded menus and some junk mail tossed in. Max's bed was made and the bathroom sink and tub were dry. She opened a few drawers in the vanity but didn't see anything out of the ordinary, just Max's shaving kit and the usual toiletries. A collection of pricy aftershaves were lined up at the edge of the counter in front of the mirror. It definitely didn't look like Max had been home recently.

"Where are you?" Penelope whispered, closing a bathroom drawer.

Her phone buzzed in her back pocket and Penelope jumped, the sound highlighting the absolute silence of the apartment. She looked at the screen and saw an unknown New York number.

"Hello?"

"Is this Penelope Sutherland? Red Carpet Catering?" the man's hurried voice said.

"Yes," Penelope answered.

"Great. This is Gary from production. Call time is five p.m. tomorrow, fifty-two people reporting to set."

Penelope put her hand to her forehead and looked in the bathroom mirror. "Right. We'll be there. How long is the day going to be?"

"Current plan is to film until morning, through the night. Twelve hours. We'll break for dinner around midnight, one o'clock."

"That late? Are you shooting exterior scenes?" Penelope asked, already doing the math in her head about how many dishes they'd need to make, when to start cooking, and how much sleep she was going to miss.

"Exterior, on the balcony, location is still The Crawford. You're in the basement." Penelope could tell he was anxious to get off the phone. He probably had several more calls to make.

"Okay, see you tomorrow night." He clicked off without saying goodbye. She was beginning to regret agreeing to this project. So far everything seemed loose and unprofessional, definitely not how she was used to working.

Irritated and distracted by the phone call, she sat down on the lid of the toilet and put her head in her hands. Underneath the counter was a small silver trash can with a few tissues inside, the corner of a pink box sticking out from underneath. She leaned over to get a closer look and her heart did a quick series of beats against her ribcage.

Penelope recognized the logo, a blue circle with the letters RPT in script, right away. Grabbing a piece of toilet paper, she reached down and gently eased the box out of the trash can, hearing the plastic wand rattle around inside. Penelope tilted the box and slid the wand out onto the countertop, watching the bright pink plus sign spin around twice before coming to a stop.

CHAPTER 14

Penelope sat on Max's couch and tried to think. The little pink plus sign from the Rapid Pregnancy Test kit she'd found in the bathroom danced before her eyes.

"Jesus, Max," Penelope said to the empty room. She shook her head and tried to think about what to do. She loved Arlena and, by extension, her brother, but she was having a hard time thinking of Max as a father. He was still so young. A partier living in New York, enjoying the privileged life of a celebrity. She could not imagine Max settling down and starting a family.

Then she thought about Hannah, her mind skimming back over what she knew about her. Her parents were famous British musicians, and former heroin addicts. Their songs were constantly on the radio when Penelope was in school. The Devores had cleaned up their act and formed a successful record label since those days and were instrumental in shaping the current music charts. They'd discovered many well-known bands, molding young talent into hit makers. But it seemed Hannah was taking after the younger version of her parents, her wild behavior constantly documented in the tabloids and online. Penelope had seen more than a few pictures of Hannah looking wasted and wearing very little clothing while out on the town, surrounded by other young celebrities with similar appetites for excess.

Penelope brushed invisible lint from her jeans and stood up, deciding Hannah deserved the benefit of the doubt. Living with Arlena, Penelope knew how the entertainment media could twist things, creating an alternate version of events. If Max loved Hannah and they had decided to start a life together, it wasn't her place to judge them.

Penelope went back into the bathroom and carefully slid the wand back into the box, repositioning it under the tissues in the trash can just the way she'd found it. She washed her hands, then went back out to the living room and straightened the throw pillows on the couch. She took one last look around before pulling the door of the apartment closed behind her and heading back down the hallway to the elevator. Her finger paused on its way to press the L button and moved instead to press R, and the elevator moved swiftly up to the roof. Penelope had watched Max's show a few times while she was making dinner at home and knew the roof was one of the main hangouts for the cast. She thought it might be worth a look to see if Max or Hannah had decided to come up last night to stargaze or talk about their future, maybe falling asleep under the glass-enclosed porch on one of the large canopy beds.

The elevator opened up to the rooftop patio and Penelope stepped off to take a look around. The oversized hot tub sat in the far corner, its cover stretched tightly over the top. A row of unoccupied lounge chairs was lined up against the wall beneath the railing, the morning sun warming the stark white cushions. Penelope walked to the railing and took in the view, barely able to make out the top of the Empire State Building in the distance. There were hundreds of buildings housing thousands of people in just the few blocks surrounding Max's building. She thought for a moment about how difficult it was to find someone in the city, to locate just one individual within the millions who called this island home. She sighed and fought back feelings of fear, and of being overwhelmed by what might have happened to Max.

She walked to the corner of the roof where a row of rosebushes sprouted from a concrete planter on the railing. She leaned down to smell one of the pink flowers and noticed a little white moth had gotten caught in an invisible spider web between two leaves. It beat its wings uselessly against the web as it tried to free itself.

Penelope reached in, swiping at the web with her finger, being careful not to prick herself on the thorny stems. The moth fluttered away quickly, its tattered wings causing it to fly jerkily as it fled from the building. Penelope watched it go until she couldn't see it anymore.

Penelope walked back to the reception desk in the lobby to sign out of Max's building.

"All quiet upstairs?" the security guard asked. He pressed his earpiece farther into his ear and leaned back in his chair.

"Yes," Penelope said, unnerved. "Max isn't home."

She picked up the pen next to the logbook and jotted down the time that blinked on the digital clock next to it. It was just past ten in the morning, and Penelope didn't feel like she was any closer to finding out what happened to Max than she was the night before.

Another security guard emerged from a doorway behind the desk. Penelope could see it led to a darkened room with a bank of security monitors on the wall. He closed the door and muttered to the man in the chair, "I'm back on the clock, Jimmy. You can head out."

Jimmy stood up and the men started talking with each other quietly, discussing their shift change and different tasks that one or the other of them would complete that day.

Penelope's eyes flicked up the sign-in sheet, looking for Max's name in the "GUEST OF" column. She didn't see any entries for him and flipped the page over to look at the previous day's log. Her eyes skimmed the rows, scanning the entries for names, times, and visitor signatures.

Jimmy reached over and closed the book, pulling it gently away from her. "Have a nice day," he said quietly.

"Thanks," Penelope stammered. "You too."

CHAPTER 15

The door to Max's building clicked shut behind her. She was back on the street, contemplating her next move. She noticed the bookstore was now open, a steady stream of people entering through the double glass doors.

A young woman with spiky blond hair and a knit hat leaned against the front window smoking a cigarette, one of her dark brown UGG boots propped up against the glass. She tossed a glance at Penelope as she exited Max's building, then studied her thumbnail, her cigarette smoldering between her fingers.

When Penelope got closer, she saw the woman was wearing a nametag around her neck, its silver chain twisted with the lanyard from her neon blue eyeglasses. According to the tag, her name was Angel Trapp and she was assistant manager of the bookstore beneath Max's building, Read it and Weep.

"Hi," Penelope said, approaching her. "Can I ask you a question?"

The woman shrugged. "Sure."

"Do you know anyone who lives in this building?"

"I guess. Maybe," Angel said, taking another drag from her cigarette. "Why?"

"I'm looking for my friend. I saw he had a couple of books upstairs. Maybe he got them here. Do you know Max Madison?" Penelope asked hopefully.

"I know Max," Angel said, nodding slowly. "He comes in all the time for his magazines. Once in a while he asks me to recommend a book. I love his dad's movies." She looked wistfully towards the street and took another drag of her cigarette. She glanced at the end of it, apparently deciding it had been smoked enough, and walked across the sidewalk to throw the remainder through a sewer grate in the gutter. She walked back to Penelope and stood, hands on her hips, glancing towards the doors of the store.

"When was the last time you saw Max?" Penelope asked. She wasn't sure what this woman could tell her, but was grateful to have someone to talk to about Max.

"Um..." Angel shifted her weight to her other hip and looked down at the sidewalk. Penelope glanced at her tights and noticed what she originally thought were polka dots were actually tiny hot pink skull and crossbones. "I'm going to say last Tuesday. He usually comes in on Tuesdays, because that's when we lay out the new book and music releases and refresh the newsstand. I can't be totally sure, but I think that was the last time he was here."

Penelope's shoulders shrank in on themselves. She had no idea what she'd hoped, that maybe Angel would tell her Max was inside the store right now, drinking a latte and reading the Sunday *Times*.

"He was with someone last time. I remember because she bought an expensive book for him. He insisted on paying for everything, but she wanted him to have it as a gift. A book of Greek plays. I had to cancel the sale and ring it up again separately." Angel patted her cigarette pack in her skirt pocket. She glanced at the door of the store again and watched a group of young hipsters enter. "I have to get back to work," she said, and turned toward the doors.

"Wait, do you remember who he was with? What did she look like?"

Angel paused for a second to think. "Blond, cute. British accent. Handsy," she said with a sly smile. "I accidently interrupted them. I came out of the bathroom and they were making out in the poetry section."

"Was it Hannah Devore, by any chance?" Penelope asked.

"Who's that?" Angel asked, genuinely at a loss.

"She lives upstairs. British. Daughter of Niles and Chastity Devore. She's on the TV show with Max."

"I don't watch TV. But yeah, I know who Niles Devore is, although I don't listen to pop music. Not sure about their daughter, but yeah, it could have been her." Angel crinkled her nose in an expression of distaste. "We've got some of Niles' CDs back in the classic rock section. The girl Max was with had long blond hair with colored highlights. But they looked like those fake extensions you just stick on for the day."

"Have you ever seen him in here with anyone else?"

Angel eyed her warily. "Are you checking up on him? You aren't one of those celebrity stalkers, are you?"

Penelope laughed sharply. "No, I'm a friend of the family, actually. I know him really well. We haven't heard from him lately and we're a little anxious about whether or not he's okay."

Angel glanced back at the street and thought for a moment. "He usually comes in by himself. Likes to get a coffee in the morning...he's always friendly."

Penelope deflated, not sure how to proceed. "Can I give you my number? Would you mind texting me or giving me a call if you happen to see him?"

Angel looked at her skeptically, her guard going back up.

"Wait," Penelope said. "I can prove I'm not crazy..." She pulled out her phone and called Arlena.

"Pen, where are you?" Arlena said.

"I'm near Max's place, and I've just met a friend of his, who also happens to be a fan of your dad. But she wants to be sure I am who I say I am, so can you talk to her for a second?" Penelope nodded at the response and handed the phone to Angel.

Angel pulled the phone up to her ear, keeping her eyes on Penelope. She said "okay" a few times then said, "Your dad, Randall Madison...how old were you when he did *Rolling Thunder*?"

Penelope could hear Arlena's tinny response, even on the busy street. Angel nodded, apparently satisfied, and handed the phone back to Penelope. "You're supposed to call her back. And you're her chef, she described you perfectly. When I see Max again, I'll get a message to you."

Penelope thanked her and scribbled her number down on a scrap of paper with a pen from her purse. "Thanks."

"No problem," Angel said before turning away. "Come in for a coffee next time you're in the neighborhood. We always have something going on at the store."

Penelope watched her go, pulling her phone from her back pocket and redialing Arlena.

"I promised that woman Dad's autograph," Arlena said. "Don't let me forget. Did you find anything at Max's place?"

"It doesn't look like Max has been home since yesterday," Penelope said, her mind flashing to the pregnancy test in the garbage can. She watched the traffic light turn red on the corner and a crowd of people cross from both sides of Bleecker Street. The city was waking up, the quiet Sunday morning slipping behind them. "I found something that's...well, I don't know how say it."

"What?" Arlena demanded.

"I found a pregnancy test in his bathroom, in the trash," Penelope said, lowering her voice. "Positive."

Arlena stayed silent for so long, Penelope thought she had lost the connection.

"Hello?"

"Sorry, yeah, um...I guess we have a lot to talk about, then," Arlena said, sounding stunned.

"I'm sorry, I don't know what it means, or who—"

"It's got to be Hannah's, right? I mean, who else could it be?" Arlena asked. "She's gotten her hooks into him, like all of Daddy's girlfriends."

Penelope thought about saying, "It takes two people to make a baby," but decided it might not be the best timing. She opted to stay silent for the moment.

Arlena recovered and said, "I talked to Daddy...he's still in the city. I gave him your number. I'll text his to you when we hang up so you can get in touch with him if you need to. Sam's about to leave for his flight, and then I'm coming in too."

"Arlena, I'm not sure what to do next."

"I had an idea. I tried calling Sienna, hoping she might be able help us find Max. Of course she didn't pick up...probably still asleep after her big night. But I got in touch with her assistant. At first he wouldn't tell me where she's staying, but when I reminded him of, you know, who I am, and that Sienna is designing a mini collection for me, he finally told me. She's at the V Hotel in Chelsea. I've been ringing the suite but there's no answer."

"I'll head over there. Maybe they all crashed at her hotel last night and are still asleep," Penelope said, a glimmer of hope lightening her mood.

"Thanks so much, Pen. I was going to go myself, but you can get there much quicker. Are you sure you don't mind doing it?"

"No, I want to help," Penelope said. "Otherwise I'd be sitting around worrying about Max or stewing about Joey. I'll head over there and call you back."

"I really love everything you do for us, Pen," Arlena said before hanging up.

CHAPTER 16

Penelope walked through the lobby of the V straight to the bank of elevators. According to Arlena, Sienna was staying in a suite on the nineteenth floor, and she intended to go directly to it and hopefully find Max, give him an earful about how much they'd all been worried about him, and head home. Afterwards, she would try and set things right with Joey. In the best-case-scenario version of how she pictured the rest of the day going, she and Joey would make it to the show and to the romantic dinner he had planned for them before everything got messed up.

The elevator rose quickly and Penelope looked down through the glass at the lobby, watching the people get smaller and smaller as she climbed. When she reached the nineteenth floor, she stepped off and followed the room number arrows to Sienna's suite.

Penelope knocked loudly on the door, then put her ear close to it to see if she could hear anyone on the other side. When she didn't sense any movement after half a minute, she knocked again, louder this time and with mounting impatience.

"Ugh," a muffled voice said from behind the door. "What?"

"Max? It's Penelope. Max, open the door," Penelope said, knocking again. Her knuckles protested as she pounded them against the hard solid wood.

The door swung open and a thin shirtless man stood before her, glaring through smudged black eyeliner. "What?" he demanded, his palms raised upwards at the ends of his long bony arms. He had a blue, red, and yellow tattoo that looked like a kidney bean on one wrist.

"Sorry," Penelope said, recognizing him as one of Sienna's runway models. He was missing his dog collar and his wave of sprayed hair had collapsed in sticky yellow clumps around his head, but she remembered him. "I'm trying to find Max Madison. Is he here?"

"Seriously? This isn't the time to be trolling for autographs or pulling some creepy stalker move." The man pressed a palm against his forehead and laughed, swinging the door closed.

Penelope stuck her foot just inside and the door bounced off of her sneaker. "I'm not a stalker, I'm a close friend. I'm trying to find Max."

The young man pulled open the door wide and glared at her again. "Right. Well, guess what, he's not here, so..." He made a sweeping motion with his hands.

Penelope stepped up on her tiptoes and looked into the suite behind him. Several full suitcases were opened on the floor in the main room, and there were clothes and swatches of material everywhere. Room service trays covered the tables, and she saw a stack of plates just inside the door next to the man's bare feet.

"Who's at the door, Jesse?" a woman asked in a gratingly raw voice.

"Sienna, it's me. Penelope Sutherland," Penelope shouted over the man's shoulder from the doorway.

"Penelope?" Sienna asked, a confused expression on her face. She came up behind Jesse and put a hand on his bare shoulder, pulling him backwards and away from the door. She was dressed in a short pink nightgown that floated around her thighs. "What are you doing here?"

"Something terrible has happened...did you hear about Christian?" Penelope asked.

Jesse reluctantly stepped aside, leaving the foyer and heading back into the suite. It was even messier than Penelope originally thought, and she cringed when she saw a half-eaten plate of pasta with red sauce teetering on the cushion of an expensive-looking white chair.

Sienna blinked at her, a look of alarm on her face. "What's happened?"

"Can I come in?" Penelope asked, glancing up and down the empty hallway of the hotel.

"Of course," Sienna said, clearing her throat. She led Penelope inside and motioned for her to sit.

"I'm sorry to tell you, but Christian is dead. Someone shot him, and now Max and Hannah might be in danger, too. At the very least, they're missing."

Penelope was exaggerating a bit, but she wanted to see how Sienna would respond.

Sienna's face reddened and she took a deep breath. Jesse hurried over and put an arm around her shoulders, perching on the arm of her chair. "Look what you've done," he said to Penelope. "You should go."

"Jesse, stop being rude," Sienna said, collecting herself. "She hasn't done anything wrong. We should try and help."

"Sienna, I'm not sure how Max is involved, but we really need to find him," Penelope urged. "I know he was there when it happened. I heard everything over the phone."

Sienna looked at her, a glimmer of hope behind her eyes. "So Max might be okay, just hiding out." Jesse continued to rub her shoulder, staring out of the room's large windows.

"How well did you know Christian?" Penelope asked, searching Sienna's face.

Sienna got up quickly without answering and hurried into the adjoining bedroom, murmuring, "Excuse me," in a hoarse whisper. When she opened the door, Penelope could see a woman's bare legs in the bed, her dark skin a sharp contrast to the white sheets draped over them. She leaned over to get a better look, but Jesse stood up and pulled the door closed before she could.

"Who is that?" Penelope asked.

"My girlfriend. I don't want to wake her up, so keep your voice down," Jesse said, walking back towards the windows.

After a few minutes, Sienna emerged from the bedroom. "I'm

so sorry. I don't know what came over me." Jesse gave her a quick hug around the shoulders and went back into the bedroom, closing the door quietly behind him.

Sienna twisted a tissue in her fingers and stared at Penelope with red-rimmed eyes. She blew her nose and glanced at the kitchenette, spotting a mug with a tea bag label dangling against its side, and went to retrieve it. Penelope smelled ginger when she brought it closer.

"Sienna," Penelope asked again. "How well did you know Christian?"

Sienna sighed and took a sip of her tea, which seemed to soothe her. "I hired him for my show through his agency. I've known him for a few months...he and all of the models met with me during that time for fittings. I've been working on this collection for months and had to make lots of alterations."

"Was he the only model you hired through that agency?" Penelope asked.

Sienna nodded distractedly, staring at something in the corner of the room. "Yes, they came from all over through recommendations. Someone showed me his portfolio online and I booked him based on that. He had the right look, exactly the kind of man I pictured when I designed the collection."

Penelope leveled her gaze at Sienna. "You only knew him through work though? You seem pretty upset about the death of someone you weren't involved with personally."

Sienna placed her mug down on the table. "My work is very personal. It's an extension of me. And it's tragic when anyone we've known is killed. It's a shock."

Penelope paused a moment to think. "Did you ever hear that Christian was involved with drugs?"

Sienna sniffed. "It's fashion. Everyone is involved with drugs. He worked as a club promoter, too. It was part of his payment sometimes."

"How do you know that? Did he tell you something specific?" Penelope urged, excited about a potential new piece of the puzzle.

Sienna nodded. "He more alluded to it, but yeah, he said that's how it works sometimes."

"Did he ever share any with you?" Penelope asked tentatively, unsure how far to step.

Sienna smiled tightly. "Of course not. I never saw anything, and for all I know he was just mouthing off, trying to impress the younger guys."

Penelope sat back and thought about what she'd said. "I can't imagine everyone in the fashion industry is on drugs, Sienna."

Sienna scoffed. "Well, of course not. But it's not like they're hard to find if you've a mind to. I don't allow it when they're working. I don't know why they do it at all, to be honest."

Penelope rubbed her temples. "If you had to guess, where do you think Max and Hannah are?" Her eyes flicked to the bedroom door.

Sienna picked up her mug and avoided Penelope's stare. "I honestly have no idea."

Penelope sat back for a moment and crossed her arms over her chest. "I saw Christian and Hannah together before your show. They were sharing a very intimate moment in the bathroom. Had you ever seen them together before?"

Sienna snapped to attention, her cheeks flushing. She looked slightly ill and held a wad of tissues up against her mouth. "No. She's only got eyes for Max, as far as I've seen. You must be mistaken."

"I don't think so," Penelope said. "I'm pretty sure it was her. It was definitely him. And it didn't seem like it was the first time they'd hooked up."

Sienna took a deep breath and waved her off.

"So, maybe they see other people. What does that have to do with anything?"

"You have to admit it's a concern when one third of a love triangle ends up dead," Penelope said.

"But that would mean Max is the guilty party. What's your theory...he went wild in a jealous rage and killed Christian?" She shook her head. "I have to lie down. I'm sorry I can't be more help right now, but I'm not feeling well."

Penelope started asking another question but Sienna held up her hand, fending her off. "Please go. If I hear from Max, I'll get in touch with Arlena."

CHAPTER 17

Penelope walked slowly back toward Max's neighborhood, oblivious to the people around her, going back over everything that had happened and wondering what to do next. She felt like Sienna wasn't saying everything she knew about Max, Christian and Hannah, but she had no idea what she might be holding back.

She pulled her phone from her back pocket and dialed Joey's number, listening to it ring until it went to his voicemail. "Hey, Joey, it's me. Give me a call, okay?"

Penelope walked a few more blocks to Westside Market, an organic farm-to-table bistro, and decided to get some lunch before walking the roughly ten blocks south to Christian's brownstone. Penelope was curious to see where they'd been the night before in the light of day. She also wanted to see if any of Christian's neighbors might have seen Max there at some point the night before, or if she might be able to learn anything else about Christian. She wasn't sure what she was doing, but she had a vague idea that if she found out more about Christian, the information might lead her to Max.

Penelope opted for a seat on the patio under the restaurant's awning, pointing to a table far away from the other diners as the hostess led her outside. She took a quick look at the brunch menu and tucked it under her plate, then dug through her purse for Officer Gomez's business card. She dialed the cell number and smiled as the waiter placed a glass of water down on the table in front of her.

"Gomez," Officer Gomez answered crisply.

"Officer Gomez, it's Penelope Sutherland."

"What can I do for you?"

Penelope took a sip of her water, sloshing a little onto her lap. "I was just wondering if there was any news about Max or Christian," she said, pressing a cloth napkin onto the wet spot on her jeans.

"News? No, there's no news," Officer Gomez said.

Penelope blew out a sigh. "Nothing at all?"

Penelope heard Officer Gomez pull the phone from her ear and swear under her breath in Spanish. When she came back on the line she said, "Penelope, I'm not the NYPD media department. I told you I'd help you if I could."

"That's why I'm calling," Penelope said, exhaustion slipping into her voice. She stared at a couple passing by on the sidewalk, holding hands and talking happily with each other, and attempted to keep from becoming emotional.

"Okay, let's do it this way," Officer Gomez said a little more kindly. It sounded like she was outside. Penelope could hear children playing in the background. "Do you have a specific question? If I can answer it for you, I will."

"Okay," Penelope said, pausing for a second to think. "Was Christian into drugs?"

"Yes. As far as we know, he was. I can tell you that because he has an arrest record, which your boyfriend could look up for you," Officer Gomez said. She added quietly, "Nothing recent."

"And he was a club promoter? And a fashion model?" Penelope asked, encouraged.

"Yes, all of those things. Also public knowledge," Officer Gomez said. She pulled the phone away from her ear again to yell something in Spanish, Penelope picking up the word *cuidadoso*.

"And he was definitely shot, and that was the cause of death?" Penelope said when she returned to the phone.

"Ah, good question. Yes, he was shot twice, but the coroner still has to make a ruling on the cause of death for it to be official.

Toxicology won't be back for at least two weeks, maybe longer than that."

Penelope remembered the model on the phone from the club who mentioned Christian offered his guests party favors at his get-togethers. "I guess he could have died of something drug related," Penelope said. "But there's no getting around the fact that someone shot him. Twice. Did they find the gun in the apartment?"

"No weapons were found, although there was a gun registered in Christian's name, same caliber as the bullets that killed him. It's possible the shooter used Christian's gun and took it with him when he fled the scene. Of course we have to confirm he was shot with his own weapon, but it looks likely."

Penelope rested her forehead heavily in her palm, trying to think. "I'm sorry to bother you on your day off," she said finally. "I'm just frustrated and I don't know what else to do."

Officer Gomez said something in Spanish again, Penelope recognizing the word *almuerzo*, which she remembered meant "lunch." She heard cheers from several small voices on the other end of the line.

"Are you with your kids?" Penelope asked.

"What makes you think that?"

Penelope shook her head. "I'll let you go. Thanks again for taking my call."

"Listen," Officer Gomez said, "I know you're trying to help your friend and I'd want to do the same thing if I were you." She lowered her voice. "I've been looking at this modeling agency for a while now, and every time I go there I get a bad feeling. I haven't been able to get them on anything, but something about it is off. No one believes me, though."

"I know how that feels. Have you ever been inside or talked to anyone there?" Penelope asked.

"I've been there a couple of times, responding to complaints from neighbors. Some uptight older lady runs the place. Joyce Alves. It's supposed to be a modeling agency, but I don't get high fashion from her. I never caught her or Christian doing anything illegal, just had to break up some loud parties. I have to keep my distance. The last time we responded to a complaint, Miss Alves called and threatened to bring a harassment suit against the department and our boss got a visit from his boss, telling us to stay away."

"Who is calling in the complaints about the parties?" Penelope asked.

"Neighbors from the block mostly. A lot of the time it's the lady next door. I gave her my card once, and now she leaves me messages about people not picking up dog poop from the sidewalk or parking in front of the fire hydrant. Her noise complaints from next door are real. She might be exaggerating about some of the other stuff."

"What does she think is going on there? And what does it have to do with Max?" Penelope said.

"I don't know. She just says there are always people coming and going at all hours of the night. It's a quiet block except for that one building. Maybe Christian was slinging drugs out of there, but we've never found any. He's either good at getting rid of them quick when we show up or he has a hiding place we haven't uncovered."

Penelope was suddenly overwhelmed by the idea of getting involved with what could be a very dangerous group of people. "That doesn't make sense. I can't believe Max would be friends with someone like that."

"Who knows what people do? Go ahead and help your friend. Just stay out of trouble."

CHAPTER 18

Penelope took a bite of bagel topped with cream cheese and smoked salmon and stared out at the small park across the street. A few people were lounging on benches or lying on blankets on the grass reading books and newspapers, while others strolled along the asphalt paths, tugging dog leashes or pushing baby strollers. It was unseasonably warm for late fall, and the city dwellers were taking advantage of the weather before being closed up inside during the coldest months. Penelope wished she was with Joey, strolling through Central Park or taking in a museum on this beautiful day.

She ate a chunk of cantaloupe, its deep sweetness reminding her of warm summer nights. She thought about the bitterly cold mornings of winter, and hoped she'd get to spend the holidays with Joey, their first Christmas as a couple. She usually tried to work as much as possible during the season to make it go by faster, but held out hope this would be a memorable one.

Her phone was lying on the table next to her plate and she swiped it to life, gazing down at the picture of the two of them.

Suddenly a text popped onto the screen. It was from her sous chef, Francis. "We have a call time for tomorrow yet?"

Penelope swiped her cheek before typing her response. "Yes, crew arriving at 5 p.m. All-nighter until 5 a.m."

The little bubble appeared on the text screen, letting her know he was typing a response. It came across: "????"

She smiled and typed, "I know. Crazy job. Can you let the others know?"

His reply: "Sure, Boss. See you then."

She typed "THX" and put her phone back on the table. She waved at the waiter as he passed by. "I'll take that mimosa after all."

He nodded and hurried back inside. Penelope replayed the phone call from Max the night before in her mind and wondered again if she'd misread the situation. She had been woken from a deep sleep, and her mind wasn't sharp when she spoke with him. Maybe she'd blown the whole thing out of proportion, and in the process had put her own needs and happiness in jeopardy. She might be able to convince herself of that, except for the persistent image in her mind of Christian's blood-soaked legs. The waiter placed the mimosa on the table in front of her.

Penelope took a sip of her drink and pulled a pen from her purse. If she thought about something else besides Max's wellbeing for a few minutes, maybe a good idea of how to proceed would come to her. She jotted down some menu ideas on a cocktail napkin, sketching out her plans for the coming week. She nodded at the waiter when he asked if she'd like another drink, eyeing her empty champagne flute. Penelope compiled her produce and pantry ordering lists and Googled a few dessert recipes she thought might pair well with the menus.

Twenty minutes later, Penelope paid her tab, leaving a healthy tip for the attentive young waiter, and made her way down the sidewalk to the corner, glancing up and down the crowded avenue. Standing at the crosswalk on the corner waiting for the light to change, she gave a quick glance at the young girl with the bright pink earbuds who had sidled up next to her. The traffic light turned yellow and Penelope went to take a step off of the curb, pausing when she noticed a cab speeding towards the intersection trying to make the light. She glanced at the young girl again, who was studying something on her phone. Penelope could hear the music coming from her earbuds and she tried to place the song, the familiar notes jarring something in her memory.

A pair of hands pushed Penelope roughly from behind, shoving her into the path of the speeding cab. Penelope heard the girl next to her scream just before everything went dark.

CHAPTER 19

Penelope opened her eyes slowly, and blinked at the white ceiling tiles a few times, but a sharp pain across her forehead convinced her to close them again. Her mouth was dry and her tongue was covered in a tangy metallic sludge. She tried opening her eyes again, squinting this time, trying to keep the throbbing in her head to a minimum. She glanced down and saw she was wearing a blue hospital gown, three drops of dried blood dotting the neckline.

She reached up to touch the spots and felt a twinge on the top of her hand. An IV had been inserted there, the connecting tube taped tightly to her skin. Clear liquid flowed through the tube from a bag hanging on a stand behind the bed. A television was suspended from the ceiling in the corner next to the window, its screen dark and reflecting the trees outside. Her head felt like it had been filled with sand. She looked down at her hand again and noticed a long remote next to it with several call buttons. She pressed the one next to a drawing of a stick figure nurse.

A few minutes later, a short woman with a kind face came through the door, pink scrubs wrapped around her body. The plastic badge clipped to her breast pocket said her name was Jan Kurtz, RN.

"You're awake," she said. "How are you feeling?" She reminded Penelope of her mom, and she guessed they were probably close in age. Nurse Kurtz placed two cool fingers on Penelope's wrist to check her pulse.

"My head hurts. Where am I?" Penelope said thickly, her tongue moving much slower than usual.

"Chelsea Medical," Jan said, flicking her eyes to the monitor above the bed. "Ambulance brought you in a few hours ago."

Penelope tried to sit up, but Nurse Kurtz placed a hand gently on her shoulder. "Stay still. The doctor will be in to talk with you shortly."

Penelope looked down at her left wrist. It had a splint and was swollen to the point that she didn't recognize it. Suddenly afraid, she tried to sit up again, her heart thudding loudly in her chest. "Someone pushed me."

"I'm going to need you to calm down. I don't want you to hurt yourself."

Penelope reluctantly relaxed against the pillow. She looked towards the door when she heard a sharp knock and saw Officer Gomez walking towards them. She was back in uniform, her hat tucked under her arm.

"What are you doing here?" Penelope asked, a fresh wave of exhaustion passing through her.

"They found my card in your purse," Officer Gomez said. She eyed Penelope's head, then glanced down at her wrist. "A bystander called 911 to report you'd been pushed, said she saw the accident."

"Accident?" Penelope asked. "It was deliberate. Not an accident."

"Right, sorry," Officer Gomez said. "What happened?"

Penelope started to respond, but then turned her head and stared out the window without saying anything.

Nurse Kurtz tucked a blanket around Penelope's legs. "I'll be right outside at the nurse's station. And I'll get you something for your headache after I talk to the doctor. Use the call button if you need anything else."

Penelope continued to stare out the window as tears slid down her cheeks.

Officer Gomez sighed and pulled a chair closer to Penelope's bed. She sat down, placed her hat in her lap and her hand on top of Penelope's. "Penelope, do remember what happened?"

Penelope squeezed her eyes closed tightly, fighting off a fresh wave of tears. She cleared her throat and said, "I was standing on the corner, waiting to cross, and someone pushed me from behind. That's all I remember."

Officer Gomez nodded. "I talked to the responding officer, and that's what the witnesses say too."

Penelope opened her eyes and looked at her. "What else did they say?"

"That it was someone in a blue hoodie, male, tall with a slight build, white. Not much more than a general description, unfortunately."

"And what? He just got away? There must have been a hundred people around me on the street. No one stopped him?"

"Looks that way. After he pushed you, the guy took off running through the park. No one chased him."

Penelope let out a harsh laugh.

"I left a message for your boyfriend," Officer Gomez said, "letting him know what happened and that you're here. The officer who responded to the incident will be in touch with you to get a statement."

"What good is that going to do? Most likely he's just going to get away with it."

"Unfortunately, there are people in this city who do these types of things. There's random violence, mental illness—"

"I was surrounded by people on that corner. There had to be a reason he picked me. Maybe I'm getting closer to finding out what happened Friday night. Christian was involved with some shady people."

"Look," Officer Gomez said, "I know you've been through a lot the past couple of days, but maybe this isn't related to Christian and Max. It could be a fluke, a random incident."

"I don't think that at all. Max is still missing, right? And Christian is dead. I know something terrible has happened to Max, but no one will listen to me or give me a straight answer."

"What do you mean? Who won't give you a straight answer?" Officer Gomez asked.

"I went to the V in Chelsea and spoke with Sienna Wentworth about Max, trying to see if she'd heard from him or knew anything about where he might be."

"Right, she's the designer. It was her show you were all at earlier. Detective Leary was going to talk with her today too."

"I broke the news to her, so I must have beat him there," Penelope said foggily.

"How did that go?" Officer Gomez said, sounding impressed. "Did you learn anything about Max's whereabouts or Christian?"

"No. Well, I started thinking that all of this might have something to do with his club promotion work. Maybe he got mixed up with someone dangerous," Penelope said.

Officer Gomez sniffed. "What, some wealthy investor didn't get enough people in the door and decided to kill the head of advertising?"

"You'd be surprised. The restaurant business in New York is competitive, and clubs are worse. I've heard stories, crazy stuff...outright intimidation and threats, property being destroyed because a new place opens up too close to a competitor. It wouldn't surprise me," Penelope said, gaining steam as she heard the idea taking shape. "Maybe Christian took payment for work he didn't do, and they came to get their money back."

"Okay, maybe," Officer Gomez said. "That's worth looking into, sure. You find out anything else?"

"Not really. There were other people there, one of the male models from the show and his girlfriend. I woke them all up, I think. Looked like they had been partying pretty hard."

Officer Gomez sat down and thought for a moment while Penelope closed her eyes, giving her head a rest.

"Someone may have decided to follow you, hurt you, like you said," Officer Gomez said. "Maybe it is someone connected with Christian."

"But who?" Penelope asked. "I barely knew Christian. Why would anyone want to hurt me on purpose?"

"You did hear him get killed over the phone, and you've been asking around about it. It doesn't have to be someone you've talked to...maybe the guy who pushed you was tipped off by a friend of a friend, someone involved in the investigation, to get you to stop asking questions."

Penelope sighed. "It's all so confusing."

Officer Gomez stared at her for a few seconds. "Maybe it's time you backed off of this. You're hurt, possibly on purpose. If you did get too close to something that someone would kill for...I don't want to find you shot dead on a floor somewhere."

A series of soft knocks on the door drew their attention to the doctor as he entered. He was flipping through screens on a tablet as he approached the bed. Without looking up, he asked, "How are you feeling?"

"Like I've been run over by a taxi," Penelope said. She'd meant it as a joke, but no one laughed.

"Luckily, you just bounced off a taxi. You hit the pavement pretty hard though." The doctor set his tablet on the bed near Penelope's feet and sanitized his hands, using the dispenser on the wall near the bed. He smiled at Penelope and placed his hands carefully around her neck, pressing gently along her jawbone.

"I'll let you go," Officer Gomez said. She stood up from the chair and nodded tightly at Penelope. "I'm going to look into some of the things you mentioned, check back in with you later."

"Denise, wait," Penelope said.

Officer Gomez paused, raising her eyebrows in mild surprise.

"Can you do me a favor and call my friend?"

"I already called him, remember?" Officer Gomez said, flashing a quick smile at Penelope, the first one she'd seen.

"No," Penelope said, feeling weak. "Not him."

CHAPTER 20

Penelope's eyes unglued themselves once more, but this time instead of ceiling tiles, she saw Arlena's face, smiling worriedly back at her from the visitor's chair.

"Thank God you're okay," Arlena said, her forehead creased with concern.

Penelope smiled. "Thank you for coming."

"Of course. Pen, I'm so sorry this happened." Arlena stood up and went to hug Penelope, being very careful not to squeeze too hard.

Penelope eased herself into a seated position, keeping her sprained wrist elevated and making sure not to bump it on the bed's railing. She'd done that when Nurse Kurtz was helping her get dressed, and bolts of lightning had raced up her arm and brought fresh tears to her eyes until the pain ebbed to a dull throb.

"I must have dozed off," Penelope said, glancing at the window. She could still see daylight, but could tell it was late afternoon from the red-orange glow. "They said I could go."

Arlena nodded. "Yes, you've been released. I'm going to take care of you."

"You don't have to do that," Penelope said. "I can manage if you just help me get my things together and get home. I'm feeling much better."

"Stop. I'm taking care of you," Arlena said sternly. She picked up the plastic bag at the foot of the hospital bed and glanced inside.

"Your purse is in here. And your shoes." She pulled out Penelope's sneakers and knelt down on the floor, sliding them onto Penelope's feet and lacing them up.

Penelope slid her purse out of the bag and dug in it with her uninjured hand for her phone. She had a few missed calls and a voicemail from an unknown number. Penelope's heart swelled in her chest and she fought back tears as she watched Arlena's long fingers tie her shoes. An unfamiliar ring sparkled on her index finger. "Where did you get that?"

Arlena flattened her hand and looked at it. It was a jade ring exactly like the one she had seen Hannah wearing at Xapa. "It's from Sienna's line. She gave it to me as a gift a while ago." She finished tying Penelope's shoes and stood up.

Nurse Kurtz entered. "How is your pain level?"

"It's better," Penelope said. "It's mostly my wrist and my ribcage."

"The wrist is a second-degree sprain, so you're going to have pain and a loss of function for a while. Your ribs on your left side are bruised, but there are no fractures. You're very lucky you didn't break any bones."

"And what about this?" Arlena asked, pointing to the purple and yellow bruise forming around Penelope's eye and across the right side of her forehead. Two butterfly bandages stretched across a gash over her eyebrow. "Does she have a concussion?"

"No, she took impact there from the pavement, but the CT scan ruled that out. Continue with the cold compresses and the bruising should subside within a week to ten days. The best thing you can do is rest. We'll schedule a follow-up for you here, or you can do it with your own doctor."

"I'll do it here," Penelope said. "I'm working nearby, so it'll be more convenient."

Nurse Kurtz looked at her with mild surprise. "You shouldn't be in a hurry to get back to work. Don't put any strain on that wrist or you'll risk nerve damage, which is much harder to recover from."

"Okay, I promise," Penelope said, sliding off the side of the bed. Arlena put out her arm for support until Penelope felt stable enough to stand on her own.

Nurse Kurtz warned Penelope again to rest, then pulled a wheelchair from right outside the door.

"I don't need that," Penelope said a bit sharply. She didn't want to be rude to the kind nurse, but the urge to walk out of the hospital under her own steam was overwhelming.

"Hospital policy," Nurse Kurtz said. "Only to the lobby, then you're free to go."

"Just sit down," Arlena said. "Can I push her?"

"Sure," Nurse Kurtz said. She got Penelope situated in the chair and put the plastic bag containing her personal items on her lap. Arlena wheeled Penelope out of the room and down the elevator to the lobby, Nurse Kurtz observing them the whole time. When they walked out the sliding glass doors in front of the hospital, a Lincoln Town Car slid up to the curb in front of them. The driver jumped out and opened the rear door, helping Penelope ease down into the seat. Arlena walked around to the other side of the car, slipping on her large sunglasses and pulling her thin sweatshirt hood up over her head.

"What hotel?" Arlena asked as she settled into her seat. "We'll get you settled, then I'm going to have to eat again. Stressing about Max is helping my weight gain, at least." She looked down at her stomach and rubbed it, as if it were any less flat than it had been a few days before.

"Tribeca Loft," Penelope said, leaning back against the leather seat and closing her eyes.

Remembering the voicemail from the unknown number on her phone, she sat up again and listened to it, surprised to hear Joey's voice. He sounded distant, and there was a lot of background noise, like he was in a restaurant or a bar.

"Penny, I just checked my messages and heard about the accident. The officer who called didn't give me any details, so I don't know what's going on. I'm upstate at the cabin, and my phone doesn't work out here. I can use the phone at the diner to get messages. There's a snow storm coming through, but I'm going to close up the cabin and get back on the road, down to you. Call me and let me know what's going on." She could hear the worried tension in his voice and her stomach tightened. She called his number and left a message, letting him know she'd been released from the hospital and was on her way back to the hotel. She finished by saying, "Hearing your voice has made me feel better. Please call me back when you can. Can't wait to see you."

The car slid away from the hospital and Penelope dropped the phone in her lap, breathing a sigh of relief, which pinched her ribcage. She put her hand lightly against her side and thought about how much worse she could have been hurt if she had fallen in front of the car instead of on top of it.

Arlena pulled out her phone and looked at the screen. "I can't believe I haven't heard from Max yet. I'm really worried about him." She dug in her purse and plucked out a bag of Peanut M&M's.

"Where did you get those?" Penelope asked, her stomach rumbling.

"Vending machine," Arlena said, popping three colorful candies in her mouth. She tilted the bag towards Penelope, who thanked her and took one.

Penelope looked at the clock on the dashboard. It was a little after five in the afternoon. "I've been out of it most of the day...there's been no news?"

"Nope. Daddy's been looking for him all day," she said through a mouthful of chocolate.

"What about Hannah?"

Arlena shook her head. "Whatever those two are up to, we have no idea."

"How are you feeling about the pregnancy test in Max's apartment?" Penelope asked.

Arlena closed her eyes and laid her head heavily against the headrest, crumpling the candy bag in her fist. She let out a single sharp laugh. "I'm having a hard time believing it's true. I mean..." She trailed off.

"I'm sorry," Penelope said. "It's none of my business. I was just looking around his apartment because we were all so worried."

Arlena shook her head. "I'm surprised, is all. And look at everything he's put us through today. You end up in the hospital, Daddy is worried sick, and I'm totally stressed out. I'm going to strangle him."

Penelope was quiet for a few beats as Arlena angrily ate a few more M&Ms. "How do you feel about Max becoming a father?"

Arlena crossed her arms tightly across her chest. "If Max wants to start a family, that's his decision. But I know my brother. I just don't think he's ready for that kind of responsibility. And with Hannah? How are the two of them going to manage a baby?"

"I thought the same thing," Penelope said. "But Max has a great heart. I'm sure he'll figure it out."

Arlena nodded reluctantly. "Yes, he is a good person. Luckily, he has the means to hire any help he needs. It's not like they won't be able to afford a nanny. Daddy will be happy...he loves babies."

"Wow, Randall Madison is going to be a grandfather," Penelope said, smiling cautiously.

Arlena rolled her eyes and laughed. "I guess that makes me Aunt Arlena."

The car pulled in front of the hotel and the driver opened the doors for them.

Arlena helped Penelope gather up her things from the room, folding her clothes and placing them in one of Penelope's gym bags Arlena had brought from the house.

When they finished packing, Penelope ducked into the bathroom for one last check to be sure she hadn't left anything behind.

Arlena's phone rang and she pulled it from her purse. "It's Daddy."

Penelope pulled the shower curtain aside and glanced at the tub, grabbing a shampoo bottle she'd left on the ledge. When she came out she saw Arlena sitting in one of the club chairs, her face an expression of grim surprise.

"What is it?" Penelope asked. She could hear Randall's voice shouting on the other end of the phone.

Arlena pulled the phone from her ear. "We've found Max. He's been arrested for murder."

CHAPTER 21

Arlena hung up with her father and stared out of the hotel window in stunned silence.

"What happened?" Penelope asked.

"He's been arrested. Daddy doesn't have all the details yet, but from what Max told him on the phone, they're charging him with Christian's murder."

Penelope walked to the table and sat down in the opposite chair facing Arlena, the small dining table in between them. "Where was he when they arrested him?"

"Somewhere in the Village," Arlena said, breaking off her stare and looking at Penelope.

"Was he with Hannah?"

"I don't know. I don't think so. Daddy didn't say," Arlena said. "He's so upset. I don't know what to do."

Penelope reached across the table with her good hand and held it out to Arlena, who reached over to take it. They sat like that for a minute while Penelope thought about what to say. "Did Randall say what evidence they have against Max?"

Arlena rubbed Penelope's fingers with her own. "No, except they had proof he was at the murder scene, and Max had blood on his clothes when they took him into custody." She released Penelope's hand and sat back in her chair, crossing her arms loosely at her waist.

"Where is he now?"

"Some precinct in Lower Manhattan," Arlena said. "Daddy is

on his way over there. With my luck, he'll punch somebody and get arrested too. And I'll be on my own to help them."

"Let's not think about that. And you're not alone. I'm here." Penelope stood up to get the purse she'd tossed onto the bed. She retrieved her phone. "I'm going to call someone who can hopefully help us."

Arlena had gone back to gazing out the window, her shoulders slumping weakly. Penelope could see she was on the verge of tears.

"Gomez."

"Hi, Denise, it's Penelope."

"Hey, how are you feeling? They release you yet?"

"Yes, I left the hospital a little while ago. Listen, we just got a call that Max has been arrested for Christian's murder. Do you know anything about it?" Penelope closed her eyes and said a silent prayer that Officer Gomez would be able to help.

"No, I hadn't heard. I'm out on patrol. Tell you what, let me make a call and I'll be back in touch."

"Okay," Penelope said, deflating a bit. "Anything you can find out, we'd really appreciate it."

"Talk to you soon," she said, and ended the call.

"I know one of the officers from the precinct. She's going to look into it and call me back," Penelope said. "I think we should go to Christian's apartment building. It's the last place we know Max was and it's surrounded by apartments. Maybe we can find something out, something that will help Max. I was on my way over there when I got hit by the cab."

"Maybe it would help," Arlena said, a glimmer of hope in her voice. "But wouldn't the police have done that already?"

Penelope's mind skipped back to tired Detective Leary who had questioned her that morning, then remembered how she'd been the first one to talk to Sienna. She shook her head and said, "They may have, but it can't hurt to go by there and see what we can find out. We're on Max's side in this, and may be the only ones right now. If we find a witness to what happened or uncover a new suspect for them to consider, it could help him."

Arlena looked at her skeptically, but eventually agreed, saying, "Well, I don't know what else to do. I guess it's better than sitting here and worrying."

In the car, Penelope searched for news of Max's arrest on her phone. It hadn't been picked up widely yet, but she did find a mention of it on one of the local New York news websites.

"How do they get this information so quickly?" Penelope asked, scrolling through the article.

"They have contacts at the police station. The minute something happens, the papers and stations get a call, especially when it involves someone famous."

Penelope saw Christian's name and a link to another article about his murder, but it too was vague and only stated the general crime and neighborhood. She found Christian's online photo portfolio that Sienna mentioned and scrolled slowly through dozens of pictures.

"Wait, Christian has the same last name as the director of the agency," Penelope said with surprise.

"Really?" Arlena asked, looking down at Penelope's phone. "That's odd."

"Maybe they're related," Penelope said. "Alves is a common name, so maybe not, but that would be a coincidence."

The Town Car pulled up in front of Christian's brownstone twenty minutes later and Penelope tucked her phone away. She glanced at the building from the car and saw someone walk past the windows of the first-floor office of MUI.

"This is where Christian lived?" Arlena asked, stepping out of the car.

"And where he was killed," Penelope said, accepting the arm of the driver as she stepped out on her side. The pain in her ribcage was more acute now, and she thought back to when she'd taken her last pain pill. Penelope watched a tall thin woman dressed all in gray walk past the window again and glance at their car. "That must be Joyce Alves. Officer Gomez told me she's met her several times. Let's go talk to her."

"Maybe she knows who really killed Christian, or has an idea at least. We need to convince her to give us a name, or go to the police," Arlena said excitedly.

"Wait a second," Penelope said, placing her hand on Arlena's forearm. "Let's not bring up Max. I think we should find out more about Christian, find something that might point us towards another suspect."

Arlena nodded. "You're right."

Penelope glanced over at the courtyard and saw a piece of yellow police tape stuck to the corner of the fence, left over from where someone had ripped it down. "We should act like we're here to talk about modeling, and then casually slip in some questions about Christian."

They climbed the steps together, Penelope holding onto Arlena's arm to steady herself. She took small sips of breath to keep the pain in her side to a minimum. Arlena pressed the button for MUI and the door buzzed open immediately.

They walked through the foyer, stepping over a pile of mail that had come in through the slot on the door before entering the reception area of the agency. A rolling suitcase was propped against the bottom step of the wooden staircase in the foyer. The woman they'd seen in the window greeted them with a welcoming smile.

"How can I help you?" Her hair, pulled back in a low bun, was black with silver strands woven through. A cashmere turtleneck sweater hung from her bony shoulders and her pants looked way too big. Penelope guessed they were the right size, she just didn't have enough flesh on her to fill them out. She eyed Penelope's injuries with interest, then spoke to Arlena. "Looking for some new talent?"

Arlena looked at Penelope, then back at the woman. "Yes, I am. Sienna Wentworth recommended your agency."

"Ah, yes, Sienna. She just had her debut, which I hear went well. I'm Joyce Alves, the director here."

"Are you usually in the office on Sunday?" Penelope asked.

Joyce laughed quietly. "You know, it feels like I'm always here. Actually, I just got back from a business trip and had to come in to check on some things. You're lucky you caught me."

"Yes, we are," Arlena said, removing her sunglasses. "Sienna is designing a collection for me and I'd like to hire some models for a private showing. I'm interested to see what you can offer."

She invited them to join her at a causal seating area set up in front of a marble fireplace with two chairs, a coffee table, and a small couch.

Joyce smiled and interlaced her fingers over her bony knee after she sat down. "Of course. If you can give me some idea of what you're looking for," she glanced at Penelope briefly then back to Arlena, a glint of recognition in her eyes, "I can better recommend some girls for you."

"There were only male models at Sienna's show, but she said you represent a variety," Arlena said. "We were introduced to one from this agency, highly recommended by Sienna."

"Christian," Penelope said, pretending to remember his name suddenly. "He said he lived here, too...invited us over for an after party." Penelope drew Joyce's attention away from Arlena briefly.

Joyce studied Penelope's face calmly and said, "Christian, yes. Unfortunately he was involved in an incident over the weekend."

"Oh? What happened?" Penelope asked, doing her best to convey surprise.

"As I mentioned, I've been travelling, but there was some kind of...well, you'll probably hear about it in the news. He was killed, by a stranger, right upstairs. Some kind of break-in, I imagine. The police don't know exactly."

Arlena sucked in a sharp breath, feigning surprise.

"How awful," Penelope said. "Were you two close?"

The woman shrugged and swept her hands out in a "who knows" motion. "Not particularly, but it's still a tragedy. He was a good tenant and employee. We didn't interact very much outside of work."

Penelope frowned and decided to lie. "When we met, I'm pretty sure he said his name was Alves, too."

The woman leaned forward and addressed Arlena, "Who are you, exactly? I was under the impression you came here looking for talent."

"I am," Arlena said sharply. "But you have to admit that's some story. If this isn't a good time—"

The front door banged open, the glass vibrating in the wooden frame, and a young girl entered the foyer. She had several white plastic bags with yellow smiley faces draped over her forearms, the weight of them pulling at the sleeves of her sweater.

Joyce's face tightened and she bit her lower lip.

The girl walked past the reception desk and froze when she saw the three of them sitting in front of the fireplace. "Miss Joyce, I'm so sorry."

"Sinay, I'm with clients. Take that in through the back. And when you're finished, bring my suitcase upstairs."

"Yes, Miss Joyce," the girl said, backing out of the room. She was frail with a dark complexion and her thick black hair was pulled into an unruly ponytail.

"Sorry about her," Joyce said after she'd gone.

Arlena waved it off. "Now, how do I go about selecting my models?"

Joyce smiled. "We can set up an appointment for you to come in and see the girls in person."

Arlena sighed and fiddled with her sunglasses in her lap. "I'm very busy, and I don't want to make an additional trip for something so..." She paused, searching for the right word. "I really should just have Sienna deal with this, or maybe I can find an agency closer to home."

Joyce sat forward in her chair. "Of course we can help you. As you may have heard from Sienna, we represent the very best models. You can preview headshots and videos of the girls walking, and then we'll set up an appointment at your home, if that's convenient, to confirm your choices in person."

Arlena glanced down the hallway past the reception desk. "Perfect. Is there somewhere we can take care of that now?"

Joyce stood up, motioning towards the hallway. "Our conference room is right this way."

Penelope pushed herself up with the help of the arm of the chair.

"This is something I can do alone," Arlena said. "You rest here until we're through."

Penelope sat back down and watched the two of them head down the hall and through the doorway on the left. A minute later, the young girl appeared from the rear of the building carrying a tray with bottles of water and mugs of coffee into the conference room. When she reemerged, pulling the door quietly behind her, she hurried back down the hall.

Penelope stood up and winced at the pain in her side, which was now on the verge of becoming unbearable. She dug in her purse for the little orange vial of pain pills from the hospital and walked down the hallway, hoping to find the kitchen and a glass of water.

Sinay jumped when Penelope entered the room, her hands submerged in sudsy water and her back to the doorway. When she saw it was Penelope, she turned around quickly. "Oh, hello, ma'am. Can I help you?" She pulled her long sleeves down to her wrists as she took quick glances at Penelope's injuries. She didn't look at Penelope directly, keeping her gaze pointed downward or just over Penelope's shoulder.

"Could I have some water please?" Penelope asked.

Sinay hurried to the refrigerator and eased it open, grabbing a bottle of water and handing it to Penelope.

"Thank you so much." She popped one of her pills in her mouth and took a healthy sip as Sinay turned back to the sink, pulling her sleeves up and getting back to her dishes. Penelope noticed the bags she'd carried in had contained a few liters of soda and several boxes of ramen noodles and macaroni and cheese. She'd wadded the plastic bags with the smiley faces into a ball on the counter.

Penelope eyed Sinay's narrow shoulders from behind and figured she couldn't be much older than sixteen. She rinsed a stack of plates and several plastic cups, placing them on a wooden drying rack on the counter.

"So, you work here?" Penelope asked after a few minutes.

Sinay's ponytail swayed against her back as she nodded, gazing at the soapy water. Penelope walked over to the counter and leaned next to her, looking at the side of her face. When she looked down into the sink she saw the girl had shiny marks on her forearms, what looked like an upraised rash on her dark brown skin.

"You should wear gloves," Penelope said before taking another sip of water. "The soap might be too harsh for your skin."

The girl pulled her hands from the sink and quickly pulled her sleeves down over her arms, water soaking through her sweater. She looked away from Penelope, holding an elbow with her opposite hand.

"Hey, I'm sorry, I didn't mean to embarrass you," Penelope said. "Your name is Sinay, right? I'm Penelope."

Sinay looked up at her timidly, pulling her wet sleeve away from her skin. "What happened to you?" she finally asked in a soft voice.

"I was in an accident," Penelope said. "I got hit by a car this morning."

Sinay's eyes moved slowly over the bruise on Penelope's forehead and the gash through her eyebrow. She reached up as if to touch Penelope's face but caught herself, snatching her hand back to her side.

"It's okay," Penelope said, smiling. She held out her splinted wrist to show the girl. "I have a sprained wrist too."

Sinay looked at the splint with interest and finally into Penelope's eyes. "Yes."

Penelope paused for a moment. "Yes, what?"

"Yes, I work here."

Sinay had an accent, but she hadn't spoken enough for Penelope to place it.

"Where are you from?" Penelope asked.

Sinay looked down at her scuffed sneakers. "Venezuela."

"Wow," Penelope said. "When did your family come here?"

Sinay kept her eyes trained on her shoes. She shook her head, stifling a cry with her hand.

"Hey," Penelope said, putting her hand lightly on the girl's arm. "I'm sorry, I shouldn't be so nosy."

Sinay wiped her cheeks and looked up at Penelope. "I've been here three years," she said, just above a whisper. "My parents died when I was little. I'm going to be a model."

"Sinay," Joyce called from the doorway.

Sinay looked over her shoulder. "Yes, Miss Joyce."

"What's the matter?" Joyce said when she saw Sinay was upset. She came over and took Sinay in her arms, hugging her close to her bony chest. Giving Penelope a disapproving glance over Sinay's shoulder, she pulled the girl away and held her at arm's length. "Sinay, it's not nothing. Tell me."

"I was just thinking about home again," she said quietly.

"Oh, sweetheart," Joyce said, hugging Sinay again. "Tell you what. Why don't you go upstairs and rest for a while? Then we'll have a nice dinner."

Sinay smiled gratefully before heading up the back stairway to the upper floor.

After she'd gone, Joyce said, "Were you looking for something?"

Penelope held up her water bottle. "Yes, I found it."

"We're going to be a little while longer. You might be more comfortable out front in the reception area." Joyce stood and stared at Penelope until she made a move towards the hallway.

"Actually, do you have any crackers? I'm feeling a little woozy," Penelope said, glancing at the wooden pantry door next to the refrigerator. There was a latch over the door with a little gold lock hanging from it.

"I'm sure we don't," Joyce said, motioning towards the hallway once again. Penelope reluctantly left the kitchen. Joyce pulled open the refrigerator and grabbed a container of half and half and the sugar bowl from the counter before following Penelope.

As she passed the conference room, Penelope felt her phone vibrate in her back pocket. She glanced over her shoulder. "I'm going outside to get some air. Let Arlena know, please."

Joyce nodded sharply before slipping inside the conference room door.

CHAPTER 22

The sun was setting and Penelope felt the air taking on a chill as she stood on the front stoop outside MUI. She held Joyce's business card by the edges, having plucked it from the holder on the reception desk on her way out. She pulled her phone up to her ear. "Denise, hey. Did you find anything out?"

Officer Gomez sighed on the other end of the line. "I talked to my partner back at the precinct. They've got Max under arrest for Christian's murder, picked him up off an anonymous tip."

"Somebody called and turned Max in? I'm telling you Max couldn't have murdered Christian. Someone is setting him up."

"So you say," Officer Gomez said. "But things don't look good for him right now. What we've got is him fleeing the scene of a crime, with the victim's blood on his clothes. That's strong evidence."

"Did you find Christian's gun?"

"Not yet."

"Then there is still more to find out. Max shouldn't have fled the scene, but what if he was scared for his life? To me, that's more likely." Penelope's stomach did a slow turn and sweat broke out on her forehead. Her knees buckled and she sat down on the steps.

"Well, luckily for him, we've got a justice system in place where he can defend himself against the charges. With his money he should be able to get a good attorney."

Penelope closed her eyes and fought the urge to get sick on the sidewalk. When she opened them again, she leaned her head against the railing, comforted by the cool metal against her forehead.

"Are you there?" Officer Gomez asked.

Penelope took a deep breath before responding. "Yes. Just not feeling the greatest."

"That's understandable. Are you resting?"

"No, we're at Christian's place. Arlena is inside the agency talking with Joyce Alves."

"She is?" Officer Gomez said, a note of excitement in her voice. "What are they talking about?"

Penelope lowered her voice and glanced behind her to make sure no one was approaching the door. "Arlena's acting like she's hiring models for a private show, but we're really trying to poke around to find out more about Christian."

Officer Gomez snorted. "You two are playing detective, huh? I told you to be careful."

"Well, we're not getting anywhere, except actually hiring some models." Penelope watched an older woman turn the corner and head towards her on the sidewalk, pushing a metal cart full of shopping bags.

"I gotta go respond to a call. You should go home and get into bed," Officer Gomez said.

"Can I call you again if I need to?" Penelope asked.

"Like I can stop you?"

"Wait, one more thing." Penelope's thoughts were fuzzy at the edges from the pain pill, but she had a sudden moment of clarity. "What was the name of the neighbor? The one who complains about the parties here?" Penelope watched the old woman stop at the neighboring brownstone and haul her cart up the stoop, one step at a time.

"Mrs. Sotheby. Just across the courtyard," Officer Gomez said. Penelope could hear her car's siren and voices talking back and forth on her radio before she abruptly ended the call.

Penelope pulled herself up with the help of the railing. She was relieved to find the pain in her side and head had lessened to a dull throb. Her nausea had passed as well, but had been replaced with a nagging hunger deep in her belly. She remembered too late Nurse Kurtz telling her she should eat something before taking her pain medication.

She looked to the right and saw the bodega was open. There were wooden crates filled with fresh fruit by the front door, and she could probably get a sandwich inside. Penelope looked back and saw Christian's neighbor had finally gotten her shopping cart to the top of the stoop and was digging around in her brown leather purse for her keys. Penelope walked over to her.

"Excuse me," Penelope said to the woman's back. She wore two homemade looking cardigan sweaters, one shade of pink apart, and a tartan plaid skirt.

The woman's shoulders stiffened and she hurried to get her key into the lock. She didn't turn around or respond.

"Mrs. Sotheby? Hi, I'm Penelope."

Mrs. Sotheby turned around slowly, her expression wary.

"I'm sorry to bother you." Penelope paused, making a quick decision to tell a white lie. "I'm working with the police to find out more about what happened here last night." Penelope glanced at the courtyard and back at Mrs. Sotheby. "I know you witnessed all the commotion. I saw you through the window."

Mrs. Sotheby cleared her throat. "I saw you too. You were under arrest, I believe."

Penelope smiled. "Yes, I was. That was a misunderstanding, as you can see." She held up her hands to show they were currently free of handcuffs.

"What happened to you? Were you hurt in the fall?" Mrs. Sotheby said, looking at Penelope's splinted wrist.

"No, I was in an accident this morning."

Mrs. Sotheby sighed. "What do you want with me?"

"Right," Penelope said, encouraged. "I was hoping you could answer some questions about what you saw."

Mrs. Sotheby hesitated, then said, "Okay, come on up. I was wondering when you all would get around to questioning the neighbors. These other ones," she glanced at the large apartment building across the street, disapproval on her face, "they never get involved. All those windows are fused shut. They could be living anywhere, no concern at all for the neighborhood."

Penelope looked at the large modern building and made a sympathetic face before climbing the stoop and following Mrs. Sotheby inside. She helped get her shopping cart over the door jam, then parked it at the bottom of the stairs once they were inside. Mrs. Sotheby fussed with her sweaters, unbuttoning the top and then the one underneath as she led Penelope inside.

"Do you live here alone?" Penelope asked, eyeing the walls of the living room. It was neat and tidy, but almost every spot was taken up by a piece of artwork or an antique mirror. Over the fireplace was a yellowing wedding picture in an oval frame, the glass bowed out to give it a fishbowl effect. A handsome young couple stared at something to the right of the camera, the man's hand resting gently on his bride's shoulder. She held a small bouquet of white flowers and smiled sweetly, happiness radiating from her face.

"Yes," Mrs. Sotheby said, glancing at the wedding picture. "My husband passed away over forty years ago."

"I'm sorry to hear that," Penelope said.

"Thank you." She pointed to an antique settee with red brocaded material stretched across the backrest. Penelope moved a needlepoint pillow out of the way and took a seat. A white cat jumped up on the cushion next to her, purring loudly. "Can I get you anything? You look a little green around the gills, if you don't mind me saying so."

"I'd love some water," Penelope said gratefully.

"Okay, I'll be right back."

Penelope watched her go down the hallway and realized Mrs. Sotheby's house had the same layout as the brownstone next door. Except this one hadn't been broken up into apartments. Penelope looked again at the walls and saw a grouping of sabres hung in the corner, their sheaths ornately engraved and colorful tassels hanging from them. Several oil paintings hung around the room, in various styles from many different eras. Penelope pulled her phone from her purse and sent Arlena a quick text that she was next door, talking with the neighbor. Noticing she had no new calls or texts from Joey, she sighed, then slipped her phone back into her purse.

Mrs. Sotheby came back a few minutes later holding a silver tray with a matching tea service. She'd included a selection of crackers and cookies and placed it on the table in front of Penelope. "I took a chance. I hope you like tea. You look like you could use a bit more than water right now, dear."

"Thank you," Penelope said, accepting a cup of tea. Mrs. Sotheby plopped a sugar cube into Penelope's cup. After it dissolved, Penelope took a sip and was immediately grateful. She couldn't remember tasting a better cup of tea in a very long time. She began to relax, the pain in her head and side ebbing away even more.

"Now, what would you like to ask me about?" Mrs. Sotheby asked, easing back in her chair, holding a matching cup. The cat jumped down from the settee and up into her lap, pawing her skirt and purring loudly.

"Who do you remember seeing next door last night? Besides me and Joey, and the man who pushed me."

"Hmm. I'd have to check my notes but no one out of the ordinary," Mrs. Sotheby said. "Just the usual."

"The usual?" Penelope asked.

"Yes, the young man who lives there and his friends. They always come home late, shouting or playing music, as if no one else could possibly hear them."

"Mrs. Sotheby, did you know that Christian was killed?"

Mrs. Sotheby looked momentarily stricken, and placed a hand over her heart. "I know, it's terrible. I didn't think he was the best neighbor in the world...but still, I was very sorry to hear he'd been killed."

Penelope placed her teacup on the table and took a sugar cookie. "Was he related to Joyce? The director of the agency?"

Mrs. Sotheby shrugged. "They must be, don't you think? They had the same last name, at least."

"When I spoke with her, she said he was her tenant and employee, didn't act like he meant much to her at all," Penelope said.

"Well, I don't know about that. But I know his name was Alves. He told me so on the street one day, and I came home and wrote it down in my file."

"Your file?" Penelope placed a half-eaten cookie on her saucer.

Mrs. Sotheby smiled. "Yes, I keep a file on everything that goes on over there. I have a lot of notes. I keep a notebook on all the buildings on the street. The police told me I couldn't keep calling them without any proof of wrongdoing, so now I keep a record of things that I see."

Penelope stared at her, her mouth hanging open. After a few seconds she said, "Where is this file, Mrs. Sotheby?"

"It's upstairs in my office. Would you like to see it?"

Penelope looked out the window of Mrs. Sotheby's office and down at the courtyard between the buildings. She had a clear view of the side door of Christian's, nothing obstructing it except a few strands of twinkly lights. Daylight was fading, but she could see the broken window pane on the door had been covered with plywood.

Mrs. Sotheby had an antique rolltop desk with various cubby holes for bills and other paperwork. Built-in bookcases lined the room in the same dark wood, filled with detective novels and books for the amateur investigator.

Penelope noticed an antique set of Arthur Conan Doyle's novels on one of the shelves. It took her a minute to realize it, but there wasn't a computer anywhere in the office, just a series of ledgers lined up in a row on the desk.

"Here it is," Mrs. Sotheby said, pulling out a thick leather book. "This is volume three on that place. I've been keeping records on the comings and goings over there for over a year." She placed the book on the desk and opened it, flipping to the most recently written pages. "Here are my notes from last night."

Penelope scanned the entry, trying to make sense of her shorthand. "What does TDM mean?"

"Tall dark-haired man," Mrs. Sotheby said.

Penelope pulled out her phone, tapping on her picture file. Forgetting for a minute she had a new phone and hadn't backed up her files yet, she scrolled over to the Google app and typed in Max's name, pulling up the first image of his face. "Is this the man you saw?"

Mrs. Sotheby pulled her glasses down her nose. "Yes, I believe that's him."

Penelope looked back down at the ledger. "It says here he arrived at eleven forty-five with a SBF...short blond female?"

Mrs. Sotheby nodded. "Yes, tiny little thing. I was on my way to bed, but they were laughing and being rowdy, so I made a note."

"Were they with anyone else?" Penelope asked.

"No, just Christian." Mrs. Sotheby began leafing through the ledger, paging back in time. "I'd seen that tall man before. I wrote it down here somewhere."

"And then you went to bed? Did you hear the gunshots?"

"Oh yes," Mrs. Sotheby said, placing her hand over her heart. "I called the police to report it, but they just drove by, didn't even get out of the car to check on the house. Then I saw you and..." She glanced down at her notes.

"Joey, Detective Baglioni."

"I guess. I saw you two poking around. Then I called Officer Gomez directly. Told her everything I'd seen and heard."

"Did you recognize the man who ran past me? The one who shoved me into the courtyard?"

"No, I couldn't see his face with that hood pulled up. And he ran away so quickly," Mrs. Sotheby said with regret.

"Wait, did you see Max and the blond girl leave after you heard the gunshots?"

"No, I didn't. I went downstairs to use the phone in the kitchen after I heard those terrible sounds. My hands were shaking so bad, I had to get one of my heart pills from the drawer."

Penelope deflated a bit, realizing Mrs. Sotheby wasn't a surveillance team, just a curious older neighbor who had partial notes and recollections of what might have happened. "Are there any other exits from the building apart from that door right there and the front door?"

"Well, there's the storm doors down to the basement, but they're always padlocked from the outside. I suppose someone could climb down from one the windows on the other side of the house without me seeing them."

Penelope sat down in the desk chair and stared at the ledger in front of her. "Would you mind if I took some notes?"

"Sure, there are a few pens in the drawer," Mrs. Sotheby said, pointing to a row of wooden drawers by Penelope's leg. She moved to the window and glanced down at the courtyard. "It's been quiet over there since last night. Not much to report."

Penelope pulled open the middle drawer and grabbed a pen, nudging aside a dark wooden box. She heard something metallic rattling inside and opened the lid. It was an old handgun, small enough to fit in Penelope's purse.

"Is this yours?" Penelope asked, eyeing the gun.

"It was my husband's," Mrs. Sotheby said. She leaned down and slid the drawer closed. "He was a private detective for an insurance company. Ironically, he didn't have it with him when he...when he might have needed it most."

Penelope looked up at her. "What happened?"

Mrs. Sotheby ran her hand across a nearby shelf, wiping away nonexistent dust. "He walked in on a robbery, by accident, at a convenience store up on the avenue. The robber killed the store clerk and my Richie. In just one minute, my life was changed forever. We'd only been married a short time when it happened."

"I'm so sorry," Penelope said. "Did they catch your husband's killer?"

"That's the thing, dear. They never caught the man who

robbed that store. It's been over forty years now. I doubt I'll ever know who killed Richie."

Penelope looked again at the row of ledgers. She thought about all the time Mrs. Sotheby had put into recording the actions of others, and wondered if the police had worked as hard to find Richie's killer. Her phone buzzed and she pulled it out of her purse.

Arlena had texted, "In the car out front whenever you're ready."

"I have to go," Penelope said. She jotted down her name and number on a slip of paper on the desk. "Here's my number. Would it be okay if I contacted you again?"

Mrs. Sotheby wrote down her own number and handed it to Penelope. "Sure, that would be fine."

Penelope took some photos of the last few pages of the ledger with her phone. "I really appreciate you letting me see all of this. I hope it helps. I'm worried an innocent man is being framed for Christian's murder."

Mrs. Sotheby shook her head sadly at Penelope. "I hate to tell you this, dear, but I haven't seen many innocent people come in or out of those doors."

CHAPTER 23

The Town Car sped away, heading back towards Tribeca.

"That woman gives me the creeps," Arlena said with a shiver.

"What do you mean?" Penelope asked.

"I don't know. She's just cold, I guess. She talks about her models like they're clothing racks instead of people."

"Not to mention being so offhand about Christian's murder. Even if he wasn't related to her and really was just an employee, a normal person would have some kind of emotional reaction to someone dying in their home, right?"

"You would think," Arlena agreed. "I did find something interesting when I sent her to get cream and sugar for my coffee. I looked through a shoebox she had tucked up on the top shelf. It was so out of place—everything else in there was sleek, manuals and catalogues." Arlena pulled a small stack of photos from her jacket pocket. "I grabbed a couple of photos from it."

Penelope looked at the pictures in Arlena's hand. One was of a group of girls in mismatched outfits, smiling at the camera. A few of them had missing teeth, so she guessed they weren't in their teens yet. "These are just kids. Where were they taken, I wonder?"

"No idea. But they remind me of the kids from those commercials on TV." Arlena flipped through a few more of them. "You know...those ads where they want you to sponsor a child from an impoverished country?"

Penelope examined another photo from the stack. "This one looks like Sinay, the girl with the groceries, but she's younger here."

"How old do you think she is now?"

"She's probably still in her mid-teens. Whatever is going on with her and Joyce seems off. One minute Sinay is afraid of her own shadow, and the next she's hugging Joyce in the kitchen like she's her mother."

"She seemed afraid and uncomfortable when she brought the coffee into our meeting."

"Maybe Joyce sponsors girls like Sinay, brings them to America and helps them find work. She said something about wanting to be a model."

"I suppose that could be it," Arlena said. She closed her eyes and pinched the bridge of her nose. "I need to eat again if I'm going to stay on this schedule."

They rode in silence for a moment before Penelope spoke again. "What should we do next? After eating?" She pulled her phone out of her purse and stared at the blank screen.

"I think you should get some rest. You look exhausted," Arlena said. "I'm taking you back to the hotel and then I'm going to meet Daddy and find out what the plan is to help Max."

"I hope he gets released soon," Penelope said.

"Daddy said he'll have to wait until tomorrow, that they don't do bail hearings on weekends. That's if he's even granted bail."

"Maybe something in this ledger will point to another suspect in Christian's murder." She pulled open the picture and enlarged it on her screen, scrolling through Saturday's page. She gave up trying to decipher Mrs. Sotheby's shorthand when her eyes began to blur over from exhaustion.

The car pulled up outside the Tribeca Loft hotel once again. Arlena helped Penelope to her room, ordering her a bowl of chicken noodle soup and a grilled cheese sandwich once they were inside. "And a pot of ginger tea, please. Can you also bring up a bed tray?"

Penelope pulled off her clothes and stood under the shower, making the water as hot as she could stand, holding her splinted arm outward to keep it dry. She did her best to pile her hair on top of her head with one hand before getting into the shower. She intended to go straight to sleep after eating. She didn't have the energy, and didn't want to ask Arlena to dry her hair before collapsing into bed. She came out of the bathroom wrapped in one of the soft white robes that were hanging on the bathroom door just as the room service waiter was knocking on the door. She got into bed and Arlena situated the tray over her legs, placing the soup and sandwich on it and propping an additional pillow behind Penelope's back to make her more comfortable.

Penelope settled into bed, feeling a wave of exhaustion come over her as she ate. She forced herself to eat every drop of the soup, even though it was a struggle to stay awake.

"Here, take another one of these before you fall asleep," Arlena said, shaking out another pain pill from the vial.

"Ugh. I hate taking those," Penelope said. "They make me feel fuzzy."

"Well, it's just temporary. It's better than being in a lot of pain, right? You'll rest easier."

"I guess," Penelope said, accepting the little pill and washing it down with some tea. "Ginger tea...that's the second time today I've heard that," Penelope said, yawning. Her eyes were slipping closed even as she fought to keep them open.

"Sienna got me into it," Arlena said, taking a sip. She reached over and grabbed the remote, flipping on the TV. "It settles your stomach. Like ginger ale, but without all the sugar."

Penelope gazed at the screen, her eyes slipping closed. Something nipped at the edge of her mind, but floated away as she fell deeper into the softness of sleep. The last thing she remembered before drifting off was Arlena tucking the blanket over her shoulders and whispering, "Goodnight, Pen."

CHAPTER 24

When Penelope woke the next morning, she was still in her robe under the blankets in the same position she had fallen asleep. She'd slept for almost ten hours, and it felt like she hadn't moved at all. She reached for her phone on the nightstand, the home screen alerting her to several texts from the night before. She scrolled through them quickly, disappointed none of them were from Joey.

The first was from Arlena. "Rest well. Call me when you wake up. I extended your room a few days and got a suite here for me & Daddy."

The next message was from Francis. "Meeting the produce order outside Crawford at 4. See you tonight." Penelope perked up at the thought of the long night ahead of her.

The next one was from Officer Gomez. "Max's GF turned herself in, being questioned by the detectives. Call me later re: Sotheby."

Right as she finished reading that, a new text popped up on her screen. It was from Arlena and simply said, "Turn on CNW. Disaster."

Penelope looked around for the remote and turned on the TV, flipping through the unfamiliar channels until she found CNW, the Celebrity News Network. She tried not to watch CNW as a rule, because their "news" and talk shows seemed to mostly involve celebrities getting ambushed coming out of clubs or being chased in airports while reporters shouted inappropriate, rude questions. Their legitimate stories were infrequent.

There was a commercial on, advertising one of their shows later in the day, but a news scroll at the bottom of the screen caught her eye. "Max Madison arrested for murder in love triangle gone bad."

"Oh no," Penelope said under her breath.

The commercial ended and a reporter came on the screen, standing outside the police station where Penelope had been the previous morning. She wore a low-cut blouse and bright red lipstick and was clearly excited to be there.

"Max Madison is in police custody awaiting a bail hearing this morning. Murder allegations have been made against Mr. Madison concerning the death of a popular Manhattan club promoter, Christian Alves. Alves had previous convictions for drug offenses and it remains to be seen if his murder is drug related, or the result of a love triangle with Max's on-again, off-again girlfriend, Hannah Devore. Several sources say Alves and Madison were both involved with Devore, a notorious party girl and daughter of Niles and Chastity Devore..."

Penelope muted the television and picked up her phone, dialing Arlena.

"Pen, how are you feeling?" Arlena asked. It sounded like she was outside and out of breath.

"Better, thanks. I just saw the news about Max." Penelope glanced up at the TV again and saw Randall's face staring back at her. The network was showing a still shot from one of his older movies, the caption beneath reading, "Famous Son Arrested."

"It's terrible," Arlena said.

"Where are you?" Penelope asked. She watched a taped segment of Randall approaching the police station, obviously from the night before, and then putting his hand over a camera lens when it got too close to his face. The shot cut to another camera's view of him smashing the first camera onto the sidewalk and pushing a reporter into a row of bushes.

"I'm heading to the courthouse now for Max's bail hearing," Arlena said.

"I got a message from Officer Gomez that they've been questioning Hannah," Penelope said. "Maybe she can help clear up what happened."

Arlena laughed harshly. "That little...she's not helping at all. She's saying Max did it, that he shot Christian out of jealousy over her."

"What?" Penelope said. Her scalp started tingling, and the sensation moved all the way down to her shoulders. "I can't believe that."

"That's what the lawyer is telling us she said. Max swears it's a lie, but it's his word against hers right now."

Penelope thought for a minute. "I saw her making out with Christian in the ladies room the night of the fashion show."

"I can't believe that little tramp. It's bad enough to lie, mess around with his feelings, but now she's playing around with murder charges."

"I know. Why would she do this?" Penelope asked.

"I don't know...look, I have to get inside before they start. Don't tell anyone else about what you saw at the club, okay? It only makes Max look guiltier. I'll call you back after I deal with Max and then Daddy."

"Was he arrested too? I just saw what happened last night on TV."

"No, thank God. The reporter said he'd press charges, but Daddy offered him money for the camera and said he'd give him an exclusive about Max. So we're okay."

Penelope was relieved at least this one thing might have gone their way.

"I'll check back with you later," Arlena said, ending the call.

Penelope made her way to the bathroom and flipped on the overhead light, looking at her face in the mirror. It was puffy from all of the sleep and medication, and the skin around her eye had darkened to blackish purple all the way around and up her forehead. The gash on her eyebrow was covered in a dark purple scab. "Lovely."

Penelope showered quickly, gently toweled her face dry, then attempted to apply enough foundation to cover the bruises on her face. When she was through, they were more light purple than dark, but it was still obvious she had taken a hit to the face. She pulled a t-shirt over her head and slipped on her last pair of clean jeans. Penelope decided she'd have to pick up some clothes if she was going to extend her stay in the city. It was a lot nicer than making the trip back and forth to New Jersey, especially with all that had been going on. Her phone buzzed in the other room just as she finished getting dressed. She hurried to answer it, her heart lifting in her chest when she saw Joey's name on the screen.

"Hello?"

"Hi, Penny, it's me," Joey said. His voice sounded strange, but she was so glad to hear from him, she put that aside.

"Joey, I've been so worried about you," Penelope said.

"I got your last message. I'm sorry I couldn't call you until I got back in a cell area. I've been stuck up in the mountains in the snow, had to pull off the road for a few hours at one point. Are you okay?"

"I'm okay now," Penelope said, relieved to be talking to him. "I sprained my wrist and bruised some ribs."

Joey was silent for a moment. "I'm worried about you, Penny."

"Where are you?"

"I'm still upstate, heading south down to you. I've been driving for a while, should be back soon depending on the roads. I got suspended from work, two weeks without pay, so I decided to take an unscheduled vacation. Then this happened to you."

"Why were you suspended?" Penelope asked.

"For firing my weapon off duty, and for being under the influence of alcohol at the time. They only have my word that I was pursuing a suspect, and that I shot him. The guy I was chasing is in the wind, and no one has come forward to turn him in. I can't even prove it happened. Unfortunately, my word doesn't mean much to them right now. They tried to give me a month's suspension, but my union rep pointed out I've never been in trouble before, so they knocked it down to two weeks."

Penelope sat down on the edge of the bed. "Joey, I'm so sorry."

Joey sighed on the other end of the phone. "It doesn't matter. What matters is that you're okay, and you're keeping yourself safe until I can get back."

After a few seconds of silence Penelope said, "I will. I miss you."

"I miss you too, Penny," Joey said. "I'll be there as soon as I can. I hate knowing you're hurt. Promise me you'll be careful."

"Yes, I promise. I really wish you were here, Joey," Penelope said, trying to keep her voice strong.

"I'm sorry I left. I was angry, and being selfish about it. It won't happen again."

"Okay, call me when you get back," Penelope said. She felt a weight had been lifted from her shoulders.

"I love you," Joey murmured before saying a quick goodbye and ending the call.

As she listened to the dead air over the phone, Penelope realized she was fighting for air, struggling to bring in a complete breath, the urge to be with him was so strong. She closed her eyes and imagined he was there holding her, protecting her from everything that was happening. She opened them again and her vision blurred behind the tears she'd been fighting.

She cleared her throat and wiped her eyes, glancing at the muted television. A series of images flashed across the screen: Max, Arlena, Randall, Hannah. She picked the remote and turned it off.

CHAPTER 25

Penelope walked through the streets of Tribeca, only vaguely noticing the people passing by her on the street. The sounds of traffic and conversation flowed around her, and she felt like a salmon swimming upstream against a current of anonymous strangers, just another soul in the crowd. She stuffed her hands into her jeans pockets, her purse bouncing lightly on her hip.

She shivered in the chilly morning air, deciding to stop in the next store she saw where she could buy a jacket or a sweatshirt. Penelope noticed a few people taking quick glances at the splint on her arm or at her poorly camouflaged bruises, but most people just looked away, unwilling to think about or get involved in problems not their own.

Penelope stopped in a clothing shop a few minutes later and bought a gray fleece jacket with a hood and I ♥ NY embroidered on the chest in pink. She pulled it on and headed into the diner next door for some breakfast. After slipping into a small booth in the back and ordering some eggs and coffee, she pulled her phone from her purse and scrolled through her recent calls to find the one from Gary on the production team.

"Yeah?" he answered, irritation in his voice.

"Gary? This is Penelope from catering."

"What do you need?"

"I've been in an accident and I'm injured. I wanted to let you know I might not be able make it through the whole night. But my team will be there, and they're more than capable of handling everything you'll need."

Gary laughed. "No, no, no. The contract says we get five chefs every filming day. Unless you have someone to replace you, we'll let you guys go and call in the next catering company down on the bid sheet to take over the job."

Penelope sat stunned. "You'd fire us because I've been in an accident and can't use my hand? You're running a small set. Four chefs are more than enough to serve dinner for fifty people."

"Whatever. If you can't fulfil the contract, we'll call someone who can."

Penelope thought about what he was saying, then about her crew. She knew Francis was putting the last bit of money together for a down payment on a new condo, and one of the others was saving up for an engagement ring. She didn't have another job lined up for them at the moment, and didn't want to cause them any financial worries.

"Fine. We'll all be there for the whole night," Penelope said, rolling her eyes. She didn't look up when the waitress set her coffee mug down in front of her.

"Call time is five." And he hung up on her once again.

"I really hate this shoot," Penelope muttered. Her head ached dully behind her eyes and her wrist twinged in the splint. She'd decided against taking another pain pill this morning, wanting to remain sharp with her thoughts clear. With everything going on, she had a brief impulse to take two and crawl back under the covers to sleep until she could see Joey again. But she would only feel worse when she woke up, and she would've lost a whole day on top of it.

After breakfast she was restless, unsure of how to spend the afternoon before going to work. She decided to walk for a while, clear her head and go over everything that happened step by step again in her mind. Without really realizing it, she had walked back toward Max's neighborhood, and decided to head to his building, in the off chance she might run into Hannah.

* * *

On her way to Max's apartment, Penelope decided to stop at the corner of her accident. She could see both the restaurant where she'd had lunch and the entrance to Max's building. She took a seat on a bench at the edge of the park and watched the traffic light change several times. Crowds of pedestrians gathered and waited, then flowed across the wide avenue with the light. She thought about how normal it all seemed, just an average street corner in Manhattan, nothing remarkable about it at all. Except for her, because it was the exact spot where someone almost took her life. Whether it was on purpose or a random act carried out by a stranger, the result was the same. Penelope had conflicting feelings of sorrow and anger, mixed with helplessness and sadness that someone could be so careless with another person's life.

She saw a young couple being buzzed in through Max's front door. She didn't recognize them from the TV show, but she also wasn't totally up on who all the stars were. Pushing herself carefully up from the bench, she moved to the crosswalk. She stood back from the curb, hanging on tightly to her purse and making sure no one was right behind her. The crosswalk light gave her the go-ahead, and she hurried across to Max's building. She pressed the buzzer and looked up at the camera in the corner.

"Can I help you?" the voice asked.

"Hi, it's Penelope Sutherland, Max's friend. Can I come in?"

The door buzzed and she pulled it open, careful not to let it bounce off her injured wrist. Jimmy had stepped out from behind the reception desk to meet her in the lobby. He gave her a concerned onceover, ending with the splint on her wrist.

"Miss Sutherland," Jimmy said. "Nice to see you again."

"Thanks."

"Max isn't here," Jimmy said, hesitation in his voice. "I don't know if you've heard, but—"

"Yes, I know he's been arrested."

Jimmy pulled his suit jacket down and crossed his arms in

front of him, holding one wrist in the opposite hand. "What happened to you, if you don't mind me asking?"

"Someone pushed me in front of a cab yesterday at the intersection just outside."

"That was you? We heard all the commotion, but I didn't realize...are you okay?"

"It could have been much worse. I was lucky."

Jimmy gave her a sympathetic nod. "Some luck. This city is nuts sometimes."

Penelope took a breath. "Jimmy, can I look at your surveillance footage from Tuesday of last week? Angel next door thinks he was in the bookstore that day with a woman. If I can prove it was someone else who..." Penelope trailed off when she realized he was already shaking his head.

"I'm sorry, Miss Sutherland, but I can't do that. I really like Max. He's one of the nice ones, never any trouble. I want to help, but I could lose my job." Jimmy paused and took another look at the bruises on Penelope's face. "Tell you what. I have a break coming up. Why don't you go next door and wait for me in the café? I'll take a look and let you know if I see anything on the tape." He looked over his shoulder at the reception desk. "I'll send the other guy upstairs for something and see what I can find."

"I really appreciate this, Jimmy. Thank you," Penelope said, walking backwards towards the door.

CHAPTER 26

Read It and Weep was crowded for a Monday morning, with most of the café tables taken up by people typing on laptops or scribbling in journals, feeding off the free Wi-Fi and jazzy world music flowing from the overhead speakers. Penelope walked through the main section of the store, glancing at various tables stacked with books. Some featured new releases and some had a theme. A table near the front window had a sign on it that read, "If you like Agatha Christie, you'll love these." A nice selection of traditional mysteries was displayed below it. She saw a table dedicated to Poe, one to Stephen King, and a larger one with young adult titles.

Penelope went to the café and squinted at the chalkboard menu suspended from the ceiling. All the coffee drinks were organic, a few of them made from beans she hadn't even heard of. "Can I get a pumpkin latte?" she asked, picking something familiar as she placed her order with the interestingly pierced and heavily tattooed barista behind the counter.

The girl smiled sweetly. "I'll bring it out to you."

"Thank you," Penelope said, thankful for the opportunity to rest. She felt stronger than the day before, but she was still functioning at about half her normal energy level. She took a seat at the most remote table she could find.

"Hello again," Angel said as she approached Penelope's table. She had a stack of magazines in the crook of her arm she had picked up from empty café tables nearby.

"Oh, hi," Penelope said. She tucked her splinted arm under the table in a feeble attempt to conceal it.

"What happened?" Angel said when she got closer.

Penelope gave up and pulled her arm out from beneath the little round table. "I got hit by a cab right out there." She pointed at the street corner.

"Wow, I heard about that. I'm so sorry that happened."

Penelope smiled, offering a thank you to the barista who dropped off her latte.

Angel called to the girl as she walked away. "Would you bring my friend a chocolate croissant please?"

Penelope began to refuse, waving her away.

"I insist. They're really good today, and you could use one." Angel set the stack of magazines on a neighboring table and pulled her leather miniskirt down over her fuzzy pink tights.

"Actually, a chocolate croissant sounds wonderful," Penelope said.

The girl returned quickly with two of the pastries on a chipped blue plate. Angel took the seat in the opposite chair and nudged it towards Penelope. "Go ahead."

Penelope took a bite of croissant. The flaky crust and deep dark chocolate melted in her mouth, instantly soothing her.

"What brings you back to the scene of the crime?" Angel asked. When Penelope rolled her eyes, placing the back of her hand over her full mouth and shaking her head, she said, "Sorry, too soon?"

Penelope swallowed, laughing despite herself. "I wanted to see where I almost got taken out by a crazy person outside your store."

"Now we have to figure out who done it." They silently chewed together for a minute.

"Actually, I'm trying to figure out if I can trace Max's steps before the other night. Before everything happened."

"You're losing me. Before what happened?"

Penelope looked at her. "Max has been arrested for murdering someone he knew, but I'm sure he didn't do it."

Angel looked surprised for a second, then nodded and took

another bite of croissant. "What makes you so sure he didn't do it?"

Penelope paused and thought for a moment, then said, "I know him, and I can't imagine he would kill anyone."

"Okay. But how well do we know anyone? Don't you think there are countless people who've said the same thing about someone who actually did commit murder? I'm sure no one thinks a close friend of theirs could do the worst thing imaginable."

"I suppose you're right," Penelope said, deflating. "But I feel certain about this."

Angel finished off her croissant. "Maybe you're right and he didn't kill this person. But you're only talking about your feelings. Do you have any way to prove what you're saying is the truth?"

"Miss Sutherland?" Jimmy walked from the café entrance to their table. He seemed so out of place in his suit, surrounded by all the hipsters.

"Hi, Jimmy," Angel said, standing up and giving him a hug.

"You two know each other?" Penelope asked.

"Jimmy's one of my best customers," Angel said. "You want the usual?"

"Absolutely," Jimmy said. After she stepped away, he took her seat. "Security work, especially in a small residential building like that, allows for a lot of downtime. They don't mind if I read behind the desk."

Penelope lowered her voice. "Did you see anything on the video from last Tuesday?"

"As a matter of fact, I did." Jimmy pulled his phone from his jacket pocket and swiped it to life, scrolling through a couple of pictures before turning it around for Penelope to see. Jimmy had taken photos of the monitor in the security room. The first picture was of Max walking through the lobby of his building, holding hands with a blond woman. She had her head turned away from the camera. Penelope thought she knew who it was already, and when she swiped to the next picture her suspicions were confirmed.

"Thanks so much for showing this to me," Penelope said.

Angel walked back over with a ceramic mug of steaming coffee and placed it on the table in front of Jimmy. "Here you go, my friend." She patted him on the shoulder and glanced at the phone in Penelope's hand.

"Angel, was this the woman you saw with Max last Tuesday?" Penelope asked, turning the phone around for her to see.

Angel bent at the waist and squinted at the screen. She pulled her glasses up from her chest and perched them on her nose, widening her eyes again. "Yep, that's her."

"Wait a second." Penelope pulled her own phone from her purse and did a quick search. "Are you sure it wasn't her?" She showed Angel the screen with a picture of Hannah's face.

Angel took both phones, holding them in each of her hands. She studied the pictures, then raised Jimmy's phone up in the air. "This is the woman I saw with him in the store."

"You said they were making out back there?" Penelope asked, glancing towards the poetry section.

Jimmy took a sip of his coffee. Angel handed him back his phone and he began scrolling through his photos again.

"Well, maybe not making out. Not with tongues or whatever. They were hugging, and she was laughing. It was definitely a private moment that I interrupted. Then she bought him the book, and they left." Angel handed Penelope back her phone.

Jimmy's phone rang. He stood up from the table, excusing himself. Angel sat back down opposite Penelope.

"Max and Sienna...I can't believe it. Why wouldn't they have said anything to anyone?" Penelope said, mostly to herself.

"Well, you said it yourself—Max has a girlfriend. I take it she's not the handsy one from the poetry section?"

"No, it's not her," Penelope said. "But I also don't know if Max's girlfriend is really his girlfriend. Sometimes it seems like they're just putting on an act for their reality show."

"I love how they're called reality shows when they're the farthest thing from reality you can get," Angel said, shaking her head. "If his costar isn't really his girlfriend, why try to hide whatever he's doing with this other woman?"

Penelope thought about Max's show, and the fact that it provided him with a steady paycheck and a place to live. "Maybe it's part of the show that he has to maintain this relationship. If that's true, I guess he'd have to keep up appearances off set too."

"And people ask me why I don't watch TV or read those trashy magazines we sell out of every week. Give me a good ghost story anthology any day," Angel said, dabbing a few croissant crumbs from the plate with her finger.

Jimmy came back to the table. "That was work. I have to get back."

"Me too," Angel said, noticing a line of people at the front register. "See you later, Jimmy." She hurried to the front of the store to help her clerks.

Once Angel was out of earshot, Jimmy perched on the edge of the chair and his face became serious. "That was my boss on the phone. We're supposed to keep Max out of the building. The show's production company is reviewing his contract, something about a morals clause."

"Morals? That's rich," Penelope said.

Jimmy grimaced. "I think they're going to wait and see what happens with the murder charge, so they're not throwing him out just yet. But the company wants to protect itself against any lawsuits from the other actors or issues they might run into by having an accused murderer living in the building."

"Great," Penelope said. "Just when I thought things couldn't get any worse."

CHAPTER 27

Penelope said goodbye to Jimmy and called Arlena from her seat in the café.

"Pen, where are you? I was just knocking on your door," Arlena said.

"Where?" Penelope asked, confused for a minute. "Oh, at the hotel. I forgot you guys were checking in."

"We're staying on the floor above yours. Max is getting released around lunchtime, after they process his bail. The judge set it at two million. Max had to surrender his passport, which seemed to bother him more than the money. You know how Max is about rules or anyone telling him what to do or where he can go."

"I know," Penelope said, thinking about Sienna and her home in London.

"Where are you?" Arlena asked again.

"I'm in the Village near Max's building," Penelope said. "In the bookstore café next door."

"What are you doing there? Have you found anything new to help Max?"

"Maybe. I'm not sure how it fits together yet, but I was thinking there must be a reason why Hannah turned on him. I'm not sure what I thought I'd find over here to be honest. Arlena, I know she's your friend, but has there ever been anything romantic between Max and Sienna that you know of?"

"No. They're good friends. I know they've been hanging out a lot while she's been in town. Why?"

"I don't know, I just started thinking about her and Max and

Hannah. The lady that works at the bookstore next to his building saw them together recently."

"They do hang out together, that's not news. He's been helping her with the fashion show. They're not dating," Arlena said with finality. "I've talked to Sienna many times over the past few months, seen her several of times too. If she were romantically involved with Max, she would have told me. Or he would have."

Penelope was unconvinced but stayed silent.

"Do you have work today?" Arlena asked.

"Yeah, call time is five," Penelope said.

"Are you feeling up to it?"

"I have to be. They threatened to fire my team if I didn't show up with them."

"What jerks. You want me to make a call for you?"

"No," Penelope said a little too loudly. She lowered her voice back down to normal. "Thank you, but I can handle it. The guys need to get paid, and I can make it through. Luckily filming will be over soon. We have a couple more weeks at the most."

"Come back to the hotel and rest before you have to go in. We're going to camp out here until we figure out what to do. Max can't go back to his apartment. Daddy hired a couple of security guys to keep any curious journalists out of the hotel." Arlena said "journalists" like it was a dirty word. "You should have seen them down there at the courthouse. Like a pack of jackals."

"Okay, I'll check in with you later," Penelope said.

Even though Arlena insisted there was nothing between Sienna and Max, Penelope knew how Max was with women. She wasn't so sure. Arlena didn't want Max dating her friends, letting him know many times that crossed a line for her. But she thought Sienna might be friendlier with Max anyway. Penelope finished her latte and thought about her next move.

Penelope took a cab to the V Hotel in Chelsea. When they pulled up out front, Penelope eased herself out of the back and looked up at the shiny glass tower, considering what she was going to say to Sienna.

As she walked down the hallway to the suite she saw a housekeeping cart outside the double doors, which were propped open with a vacuum cleaner.

"Hello?" Penelope said, wrapping her knuckles lightly on the door. A soap opera was playing loudly on the television and a pile of sheets and towels was in the middle of the floor. The smell of disinfectant wafted through the air of the suite. "Hello?" Penelope said, louder this time.

The maid emerged from the bathroom, yellow gloves up to her elbows. "Yes, miss, can I help?"

"Hi," Penelope said, stepping inside. All of the clothes that had been flung around the room were gone, and the bedroom doors were open, the beds stripped bare. "Are they gone?"

The maid pulled off her gloves and muted the television. "Yes, checked out."

Penelope glanced around the room, trying to think. "When?" she finally asked.

"This morning."

"Do you know how many people were staying here?" Penelope asked. "It was the British woman and the blond man, and another girl, right?"

The maid shrugged apologetically. "I'm not sure." She looked over at the muted television.

Penelope thanked her and left, deciding to see if she could get more information about Sienna's abrupt departure from the front desk. She stepped back off the elevator in the lobby and approached the smiling woman in the green blazer. "Hello, can you tell me when one of your guests checked out?"

The hotel clerk looked at her a bit warily but agreed. "Let me see if I can help you."

"Sienna Wentworth, Suite 1912?"

The woman typed on her keyboard. "Miss Wentworth has checked out as of this morning."

"Did she say where she was going?" Penelope asked. The woman looked at her with a confused look. "No, we don't capture that information."

"So she didn't mention anything in passing?" The clerk shook her head, glancing past Penelope into the lobby. "Is there anything else I can assist you with today?"

"Do you know the names of the other guests in Sienna's suite? I'm curious about who was staying here with her." The clerk's expression became closed. "I'm afraid I can't give out that information. We value the privacy of our guests." She sounded like she was reading off of the hotel brochure.

Penelope sighed and headed back outside, checking her phone for the time. It was already late in the afternoon, so she figured she'd have to head to work before long. She really hoped she could make it through the night. She dialed Arlena and left a message, asking her to call Sienna. Maybe she would be able to find out where she'd gone off to.

CHAPTER 28

Penelope shrugged her chef coat over her shoulder and carefully slid her splinted wrist through the sleeve. She thought about taking off the splint while she was in the kitchen, but worried if she hurt her wrist any further it would be too painful to continue working. Luckily her sleeve stretched over it without too much trouble.

After the security guard had unlocked the front doors and let her into the lobby of the Crawford, she'd popped into the ladies' room to check how her makeup was holding up against her bruised face. Some of it had worn off, so she reapplied the cool liquid to her eye and up her forehead. She couldn't completely cover everything, but wanted to hide as much of it as possible. Mostly satisfied with her appearance, she rode the creaking elevator down to the kitchen in the basement, rehearsing the story she would tell her team about her injuries.

The first person she saw was her sous chef, Francis. He stood in front of the elevator doors, carrying a stack of sheet pans from the rolling racks over to his station. He froze, his mouth falling open.

"What happened, Boss?" he asked, his surprise turning immediately to concern.

"Guys, gather round, okay?" She motioned the other chefs over. When they'd all assembled she said, "I was hit by a cab yesterday and I sprained my wrist. I'm okay. It looks worse than it is, but I'm going to need your help to get through the next couple of services."

"You sure you should be here? We can handle things," Francis said.

"That's not an option right now. We committed to this job, and we have to stick together."

They all agreed, and Francis said, "We got your back, Boss."

"I know I can always count on you guys, and that means a lot," Penelope said, making eye contact with each of them. "Here's the plan for tonight. They're going to be filming until morning and don't have a specific break time yet, which tells me they don't know when dinner will be. I say we put out some of our best comfort food. It will get us all through the night and will keep well through whatever window they give us. Let's do our turkey chili, a choice of soups, and we can do Francis's Gruyere and Gouda mac and cheese he came up with on the last movie. And Red Carpet S'mores for dessert. They're always a crowd pleaser."

After they'd settled on the menu, Penelope's team took their stations, chopping vegetables to begin the base for soups. They decided on creamy tomato basil, spicy black bean, and shredded rotisserie chicken with noodles, lemon and kale. Francis found three big soup pans and they got to work, settling into their familiar roles. The harmony Penelope found among her team in the kitchen soothed her, and she realized she felt safe for the first time in days.

Penelope took the elevator upstairs to check on the set, see where they'd be setting up for lunch. The doors slid open and Penelope realized the cameras were rolling, and she'd almost walked out onto a live scene.

"You mustn't fret, dear. You're the only man for me and you know it."

A young redheaded actress in a vintage evening gown held a smoldering cigarette at the end of a long black holder, her hair sprayed into place in a series of silky waves. Next to her was an older man in a suit, seated in a tall leather chair behind a desk, eying her suspiciously.

The elevator door began to close and Penelope stuck out her uninjured hand to stop it, silently holding it open.

"Honestly, dear, I don't know what gave you the idea about me and Randolph. It's preposterous, I tell you," the woman said.

"You're a damn liar," the man boomed. He stood up suddenly from his chair and swept everything off of the desk onto the floor. A fan of papers fluttered through the air and a water glass smashed against the hardwood floor.

Penelope held her breath and remained frozen in place.

The man leaned across the desk, propped his bulk on one thick fist, and pointed angrily at the woman, rage etched across his face. "I knew the minute I married you I'd regret it and I was right. You're a common tart. A trollop," he sputtered.

Penelope could see the director around the corner from the elevator alcove, sitting in a chair and staring intently into a monitor, his face lit blue from the screen. He apparently hadn't noticed the elevator door opening, or he did and didn't want to cut the scene. Penelope hoped she was out of camera range.

"Now darling, you mustn't say such things. I'm a good wife to you, and you'd do well to remember that," the woman said, standing her ground against her much larger costar.

The man's face reddened and he spat, "I should have known marrying a showgirl would bring a life of misery. What was I thinking? You won't get one more dime out of me if I find out you've been cavorting with that Frenchman." He glared at her and retook his seat, unbuttoning his jacket and straightening his lapels.

"And cut!" the director yelled from his chair. "Great work, guys."

"Can you tell him not to spit so much?" the actress shouted. Her voice had changed from vintage and sweet to modern and grating.

"Sorry. I was just feeling the moment," the man said, smiling widely at her.

The actress swiped at her cheeks with her hands and glared at him. A few crew members moved in to reset the scene, picking up scattered papers and sweeping up broken glass.

"Everyone take five," the director said. He walked through the set, pulling his phone up to his ear and ignoring the key grip who attempted to speak with him.

"Five minutes people!" the assistant director yelled. He waved enthusiastically at Penelope, who was still waiting in the elevator. "Catering can set up lunch over there today." He nodded towards a cluster of tables draped in white at the far end of the room, then started talking to someone on his headset, shaking his head as he walked away. Penelope let the elevator doors close and rode back down the basement.

After they'd set up lunch in the penthouse, the smell of their soups filled the air and revived the crew. The actors and crew members swarmed the table, ladling the chili and soup into their bowls and tearing off big pieces of French bread to go with it.

When everyone had been served, Penelope sent Francis down to bring up the desserts and coffee urns from the basement.

"We have Red Carpet S'mores coming," Penelope announced to the room. A few members of the crew glanced up from their bowls, mild interest on their faces. "And lots of coffee."

"Everyone give Penelope a hand," the director said, leading the room in a smattering of applause. Penelope smiled and helped clear a space when Francis returned with the desserts.

Penelope's phone buzzed in her back pocket and she pulled it out, glancing at the screen. "Hi, Arlena. You're up late."

"I wanted to check on you to make sure you're okay over there."

"Yes, I'm making my way through," Penelope said. She watched a few crew members wander up to the table and fill their plates with sweets.

"I'm sending a car for you when you get off," Arlena said.

"Thanks, but I can get a cab," Penelope said.

"No, it will be easier. I told the driver to wait for you outside. He'll be there at five and wait for you until you get off."

"I appreciate it. How's Max doing?"

"He's been sleeping a lot. He's in the bedroom now, passed out. Daddy and I have been up talking with the lawyer about his case, but we're about to turn in too."

"Did he say anything about what happened at Christian's?" Penelope asked.

"He keeps saying he will, but he isn't ready to talk to us right now. He says he's too traumatized and needs time to think."

The assistant director yelled from behind her. "Twenty minutes, people!"

"Can I stop by in the morning and see him?" Penelope asked. She looked at Francis and he nodded, understanding she wanted him to begin clearing the tables. He signaled the others and they began wrapping up the leftovers.

"Of course you can," Arlena said. "Maybe he'll talk to you."

CHAPTER 29

Penelope made it back to her hotel room just after seven in the morning. The movie's director had insisted on running through the previous night's scene eighteen times, and when they were all done, the crew was exhausted. They had burned through several three-gallon coffee urn refills and all of the desserts before he called a wrap on the final take. Penelope was glad she wasn't the main actress, getting spittle sprayed by her costar for hours on end.

Penelope hopped in the shower, removing the splint from her wrist. The swelling had gone down, but it was still tender to the touch and she'd need to be careful with it. She stepped out of the bathroom, her hair wrapped in a towel, and looked around the room for some clothes. She didn't find anything in her gym bag, and pulled open the drawer next to the wall unit. She found a selection of clean clothes from her closet back in New Jersey. She smiled as she pulled out a pair of jeans, figuring Arlena must have sent for her things and unpacked them for her. The Madisons were wonderful, even though their lives contained a greater amount of drama than the average family.

Penelope dressed and dried her hair awkwardly with one hand, then took the elevator up to Arlena's suite. She was dying to talk to Max about Sienna, and the night of Christian's murder. She knocked on the door and heard Randall say, "Yeah, I'm coming," came from the other side.

"Good morning," Penelope said when he opened the door.

Randall smiled at her, but his eyes were heavy with sadness.

"Come in, Pen." He led her through the foyer and into the living room, where he must've been resting on the couch. A blanket had been tossed aside and the television was set to the local news channel on mute. "Arlena's up. She'll be out in a minute."

"How's Max doing?"

"Okay, I guess. Jail scared him. He looked terrible when he got out." Randall walked to one of the bedroom doors and knocked loudly. "Maximilian, time to get up."

Arlena came out from the opposite hallway, tucking a t-shirt into the waistband of her jeans. "Pen, you look like you feel better today."

"Max, get up," Randall yelled again. He turned to look at Arlena, concern darkening his face. He tried the doorknob, but the bedroom door was locked. "Max," Randall shouted. "Open the door, son."

Randall gripped the doorknob and tried to force it. When it didn't budge, he braced his shoulder and butted the door, popping it open. Penelope and Arlena stood behind him as they all looked inside the empty bedroom. The bed had been made, the sheets pulled up over the pillows. There was a folded note on the comforter, and Randall hurried inside to snatch it up. "Sorry, Dad, I messed up. I hope you can forgive me. Max."

Randall's arm fell to his side and the note slipped from his hand onto the floor.

"How did he get out without anyone noticing?" Penelope asked. "I thought you had a security person."

"He must have slipped past me when I fell asleep on the couch," Randall said. "We have a guy down in the lobby, but he's just looking to keep the press out. He wouldn't have stopped Max from leaving."

"And he could have deliberately avoided the security person or used a different exit," Penelope said, thinking out loud.

"Where do you think he's gone?" Arlena said. They stood in the living room, not moving.

"I have no idea," Randall said.

"He can't go to his apartment," Penelope said. "The security team there has instructions to keep him out."

Arlena nodded. "He mentioned that last night. He was pretty upset about that, about everything really."

"Let's call him," Randall said, looking around the living room for his phone. He found it under the blanket on the couch and dialed Max's number. He shook his head. "It's just ringing. He's not picking up. Max, it's Dad. Give me a call. We just want to know that you're okay."

"What do you think he meant by his note, that he messed up? You don't think he did this?" Arlena asked, her voice going up an octave.

"Of course he didn't," Randall said tersely.

"He could be talking about everything going on," Penelope said. "Maybe he's depressed, or overwhelmed. Who wouldn't be? What exactly did Hannah say happened?"

Randall scoffed. "She's claiming Max shot Christian in a jealous rage after he caught them together at the apartment."

"But that doesn't make any sense, does it? Didn't they all go over there together?" Penelope pulled her phone from her back pocket and scrolled through her pictures until she found the ones of Mrs. Sotheby's ledger on the night of the murder. "The lady next door keeps a record of the comings and goings at Christian's apartment, or at least what she could see when she was awake and looking out the window. Based on this entry, Max, Hannah, and Christian arrived together."

"Why is the neighbor keeping tabs on the place?" Randall asked, squinting at the photo.

"She's noticed a lot of suspicious activity over there, strangers visiting all the time. The police tell her she needs specific complaints for them to do anything, so she takes notes. I think she's a little lonely too. It gives her something to do."

"We have to get Hannah to tell the truth somehow," Arlena said. "Let's go talk to her."

"I've been to Max's building and it's pretty secure. If she

doesn't want to see us, it won't be easy to get upstairs to talk to her," Penelope said. "I suppose we could wait for her outside."

Arlena sighed. "That doesn't sound practical. I'm just going to go there and insist she talk to me."

"Maybe Jimmy, the security guard I've become friendly with, would call me when he sees her leave. You could run into her that way."

"Maybe," Arlena said doubtfully. Penelope recognized that Arlena struggled at times when she didn't immediately get what she wanted.

"You should stay here in case Max comes back to the hotel," Penelope said to Randall. "I'm going to pay another visit to Mrs. Sotheby and confirm she saw them all arrive together."

"Aren't you tired? You've been up all night," Arlena said, taking a closer look at Penelope's bruised face. The purple had faded a bit, and her eye had taken on a more orange hue.

"I can rest this afternoon. I'm too amped up now to sleep, anyway."

CHAPTER 30

Penelope rang Mrs. Sotheby's bell and glanced through the glass windows of her front door. She hadn't called first, taking a chance she would be home. She saw movement in the back of the house, then Mrs. Sotheby appeared in the hallway, wiping her hands on a tea towel. She smiled when she saw Penelope at the door.

"I'm glad it's you and not some salesperson," Mrs. Sotheby said, welcoming Penelope inside. "They always seem to ring the doorbell when I'm doing my baking. How are you feeling?"

Penelope followed Mrs. Sotheby into the foyer, instantly soothed by the scents of vanilla and sugar. "I'm doing better. I hope I'm not calling at a bad time," she said as they entered the kitchen.

"No, it's a good time. I'm baking cookies for the church social tonight. It's a senior singles party."

"I see," Penelope said, taking a seat at the kitchen table. It and the matching chairs were vintage red Formica with cushions lined with silver piping. They would be perfect in a diner from the 1950s. "That sounds fun."

Mrs. Sotheby fussed over her cookie pans, opening the oven to check on the batch inside. "Well, I suppose. It's always the same old people though. But we do have fun talking together. There's usually one man for every four ladies. Sometimes I think they just come for the cookies and punch, not to really meet anyone."

Penelope smiled when Mrs. Sotheby sat a plate full of cookies on the table in front of her. "How about some tea, Penelope?"

When Penelope nodded enthusiastically, Mrs. Sotheby turned back to the stove to light the flame under the kettle. "What brings you here today?" she said over her shoulder from the sink as she filled the red teapot. "I know it's not just to chat with me over tea and cookies."

"I was hoping to get another look at your ledgers," Penelope said. "To check on the timeline of when you saw my friend and his girlfriend coming and going."

"I'm happy to help if I can," Mrs. Sotheby said. "Are you feeling well enough to go upstairs and get them? We can look at them down here at the table."

"Sure," Penelope said. "I'll be right back."

Penelope made her way up the wide staircase slowly, looking at a few of the photos that Mrs. Sotheby had hung on the walls. She noticed there were several family pictures, a few of her as a young woman with what must have been her parents. There were some casual shots with Mrs. Sotheby and her husband, who Penelope could tell was quite handsome. She entered Mrs. Sotheby's office and went to the desk, running her finger across the leather spines of the ledgers lined up under the window. She pulled the one they had already looked at and the one next to it, which contained some older entries.

A flash of movement outside the window caught her eye, and she looked down at the courtyard. Sinay had come around from the back of the house, pulling a rolling cart stacked with laundry bags. She paused at one of the tables and glanced around, appearing to be looking for something. Just then a young man entered the courtyard through the iron gate. He was carrying some plastic shopping bags with yellow smiley faces on them in one hand. He walked closer to her and placed them on the table. Penelope recognized the bags as the same ones Sinay unloaded in the kitchen the day before.

Penelope watched them speak to each other for a moment, noticing that Sinay seemed relaxed and happy around him, much different from how she remembered her being when they spoke. He leaned down and kissed her on the lips. Sinay stood on her tiptoes and kissed him back, placing a hand on his shoulder.

They suddenly jerked apart and he turned to go, hurrying out of the courtyard just as the side door opened. Joyce leaned out, motioning for Sinay to come inside. Sinay gathered up the shopping bags and climbed the stoop, leaving the laundry in the courtyard. She pulled the door gently closed behind her.

Penelope walked back downstairs to the kitchen, the ledgers tucked under her arm. She'd decided to keep her splint off this morning, and gently moved her wrist back and forth, testing the edges of her pain. She had more mobility today, but she still didn't want to put any pressure on it.

"Oh, you found them, good," Mrs. Sotheby said. "What kind of tea would you like?"

Penelope looked at the choices and chose English Breakfast. She was starting to fade from her long night of work and decided a jolt of caffeine would do her good. "I usually drink herbal tea, but I need to stay awake."

"I don't have too many of those. I'm a purist, I suppose. Give me a nice strong English tea any day," Mrs. Sotheby said, filling her mug with hot water.

"I've been drinking ginger tea lately. It seems like everyone is," Penelope said, dunking her tea bag in the water.

"Oh, I haven't had that in years," Mrs. Sotheby said. "I can't stand the taste of it. It reminds me of being sick. It does help the nausea, though."

Something clicked in Penelope's mind, and she made a mental note to mention it to Arlena. She opened the ledger to the page from the night of the murder. "This entry here is when you saw Max and Hannah go inside the apartment with Christian. Correct?"

"Yes, they all arrived together. Then I fell asleep, so I don't have any notes until I heard the shots and saw all of the commotion with you shortly after," Mrs. Sotheby said.

"Good. That's at least one potential lie Hannah is telling."

"Who is Hannah?"

"She's Max's girlfriend, the one who was there with them that night. And you said you didn't see the man who pushed past me."

Mrs. Sotheby nodded slowly, blowing on her tea. "I had left my glasses downstairs, but I didn't get a look at his face either way. I just remember his bright red running shoes."

Penelope turned back a few pages. "What are all of these entries that say YHF?"

"That's Young Hispanic Female," Mrs. Sotheby said. "Christian had a type. So many girls like that coming and going from the building."

"Maybe they were part of his groups of models, who he brought around to the different clubs he was promoting," Penelope said.

"I don't know...some of the girls I've seen, I think they're too young to go to clubs," Mrs. Sotheby said doubtfully.

Penelope put her chin in her palm and stared at the ledger. After a minute she said, "Do you have any sugar? I don't usually take it but I'm feeling kind of woozy again." Penelope remembered Mrs. Sotheby's sugary tea and how it had revived her the day before.

"Sure, help yourself," Mrs. Sotheby said, jumping up to turn off the buzzer on the oven and pull another batch of cookies from inside.

Penelope went to the door next to the refrigerator and pulled it open. Instead of a pantry stocked with dried goods and cans, she saw a staircase leading down. She gazed down the darkened stairway, confused. "I thought this was your pantry."

"No, that leads to the basement. The pantry is out in the hall, but you can just use the sugar bowl on the counter."

As Penelope gazed into the darkness, her mind slipped back to the day before, standing in the kitchen talking to Sinay. She pictured the red door next to the refrigerator, and she remembered the padlock she thought was being used to keep people away from the food. "Can I take a look downstairs?" Penelope asked.

"Sure, just be careful. Put the light on."

Penelope eased open the door and started down the stairs, flipping on the light switch right inside the door. The air was slightly damp, but not unpleasant, and the earthy smell of the basement grew stronger the farther down she went. The wooden stairs groaned under her feet, until she stepped onto the concrete floor at the bottom.

The walls were lined with shelves where Mrs. Sotheby had placed several sets of mason jars containing pickles, tomatoes, and some preserves. A new-looking washer and dryer set was pushed up against the far wall, and a few pieces of laundry tossed in a wicker basket sat on top. Penelope's saw there were four stone steps leading up to the storm doors out onto the patio.

Penelope climbed back up the wooden stairs to the kitchen. "Mrs. Sotheby, have you ever seen anyone come in or out of those storm doors in the courtyard next door?"

Mrs. Sotheby thought for a moment, rubbing her chin thoughtfully with one finger. "I haven't, now that you mention it. It's always locked, which isn't unusual in the city. You don't want people getting into your house through the basement doors."

"Right," Penelope said. "That makes sense." She thought about the photos Arlena had found and about the plastic plates and cups Sinay had been washing in the sink. "Excuse me for a minute. I'm going to step out and make a call."

Mrs. Sotheby nodded. Her oven timer went off again and she rotated the cookie sheets in the oven.

Penelope walked down Mrs. Sotheby's front stoop and over to the edge of the courtyard. The laundry cart was still outside, but it was otherwise deserted.

"Gomez," Officer Gomez answered crisply.

"It's Penelope. I'm at Christian's place. Actually, I'm next door visiting Mrs. Sotheby. Are you close by?"

"Kind of. I'm in the neighborhood."

"I have an idea of what might be going on at the agency, but I'm not sure what to do."

"What are you talking about?" Officer Gomez asked, her voice wary.

"I think the modeling agency is a front for something else. I think they may be trafficking young girls out of there, and that they're keeping them down in the basement."

"What?" Officer Gomez said sharply. "What did you see? Do you have any proof?"

"I didn't actually see anything. It's just a theory, but it might explain some photos of the young girls Arlena found in Joyce's office. I met Joyce's house girl, or whatever she is, who is also very young. She was washing a bunch of plates and cups the other day. I didn't think about it at the time, but Mrs. Alves had been travelling, and it was a lot of dishes for just one person to use, even for the whole weekend. The door leading down to the basement is locked from the outside, and the storm doors are padlocked."

Officer Gomez sighed. "Let's say your theory is correct. I can't do anything about it unless I have a complaint or a warrant to search the property, which I don't have and won't get without solid evidence."

"But Mrs. Sotheby complains about the house all the time," Penelope said.

"Has she seen anyone taking underage girls in or out of the basement?"

"No. But maybe they do it late at night so the neighbors don't see."

"I got pulled aside by my captain today. Joyce Alves called in on us again, said we were at her property harassing her. It's a lie, but she's got some kind of pull in the department."

Penelope considered that for a moment. "It would make sense for her to have some kind of protection from inside the police department. Maybe she pays to get people to look the other way?"

"You've been watching too many movies, Penelope."

"Look," Penelope said. "You know a lot more than me about the law, but I know there's something wrong going on in that house."

"Maybe. But that doesn't get me anywhere. I need some proof. You haven't seen anything or told me anything I can use."

"Let me see what else I can find out and call you back."

"Penelope, don't get yourself into trouble. I don't want you getting hurt again."

"Gotta go," Penelope said and hurriedly hung up. Sinay had come back out the side door to retrieve the laundry cart. She looked around cautiously and rolled it towards the sidewalk.

Penelope followed her at a distance as she walked towards the avenue, wheeling the cart along the bumpy sidewalk. She parked it outside the bodega and went inside, Penelope following her in a few seconds later.

The small convenience store smelled like coffee and cold cuts, and Middle Eastern music was playing from somewhere in the back. Penelope walked down the first aisle and grabbed a bottle of ibuprofen while casually scanning the store for Sinay. She finally spotted her in the back in front of the beverage coolers. The young man she had seen in the courtyard was with her again. They were whispering to each other in the corner.

"Hi, Sinay," Penelope said, walking towards them.

The young man turned away quickly and walked towards the front of the store.

Sinay looked at her, a worried expression on her face. "What are you doing here?"

Penelope held up the bottle of pain medicine. "Just needed these. I was visiting your neighbor." She glanced towards the front counter and saw the boy had taken the spot behind the register, ringing up a man who had stopped in for a pack of cigarettes. "Is he your boyfriend?"

Sinay blushed and looked at her shoes. "Yes," she said in a small voice. "Please don't tell Miss Joyce." She looked up into Penelope's eyes. "I'm not allowed."

"I won't say anything," Penelope assured her. "Sinay, have you been down in the basement at Miss Joyce's?"

She looked down at the floor again and nodded her head.

"Sinay, what's in the basement?"

"That's where we stay, it's our room," she whispered.

"Who stays down there?" Penelope asked quietly.

"Just the girls who come and stay for a while until they get work."

"But you went upstairs yesterday to lie down," Penelope said softly. "Your room isn't upstairs?"

"Sometimes Miss Joyce lets me take naps upstairs on a cot if I get all my work done."

"Can I help you, ma'am?" The young man approached them and pulled Sinay by the arm to stand behind him. "Are you having trouble finding something?"

"No," Penelope said, looking around his shoulder at Sinay. When he moved to completely block her from view, Penelope looked up into his face. He was sweating profusely, the neck of his shirt and armpits damp despite the cool weather. "Are you okay? You look ill."

He gave her an angry glance. "I think you should leave. Sinay doesn't want to talk to anyone."

Penelope tried again to look around him at Sinay, but he took a step closer and blocked her again.

"Excuse me, but she can answer for herself. Sinay?" Penelope put her hand on his upper arm to gently push him aside. She felt something under his sleeve and pressed harder. It was a bandage wrapped tightly around his bicep. She looked down, saw red tennis shoes, then looked back up at his sweaty face.

He held her stare for a second, then turned and bolted towards the door, knocking over a few bags of potato chips from the nearby shelf.

"Adir!" Sinay shouted as he ran.

Penelope took off after him, skidding out of the doorway and heading right. She chased him down the avenue as he ducked around a few people on the sidewalk.

"Stop! Adir!" Penelope shouted as she ran. She kept her injured wrist tight against her body so as not to bump it or catch it on anything. It began to throb with each step, but she pressed on, keeping his head in sight as she ran.

A police siren blipped behind her and a familiar voice came

over the loudspeaker. "Police! Stop!" Officer Gomez sped past Penelope and turned the next corner, cutting Adir off. He pulled up and stopped, putting his hands on his knees for a second, then collapsing onto the sidewalk. Penelope ran up behind him just as Officer Gomez emerged from the car and walked towards them from the opposite direction. They stood over Adir, who panted loudly and held his bandaged bicep with his opposite hand, writhing in pain on the sidewalk.

"Who is this?" Officer Gomez asked as she knelt down to get a better look at his face.

"This is Adir, boyfriend of Joyce Alves's housekeeper, Sinay. He works in the bodega," Penelope said, regaining her normal breathing. Her head and wrist ached in protest.

"And why were you chasing him?" Officer Gomez asked, a confused expression on her face.

"He's the one who pushed me out the door the other night. He's the one Joey shot."

CHAPTER 31

Officer Gomez stood at the counter of the bodega talking to Adir's uncle, the store's owner. Penelope, Adir, and Sinay watched them through the doorway of the stockroom, picking up on a few words here and there. They had pulled Sinay's laundry cart inside and shut the door, flipping the sign to CLOSED.

"Why did you run from me?" Penelope asked Adir.

He sat on a tall stool, holding his injured arm and rocking back and forth slightly. Sinay watched him with quiet alarm, clearly overwhelmed by everything that was happening. His face was pale, his brown skin taking on a greenish hue under his eyes.

"I don't have to say anything to you." He sneered. "You're just another rich housewife who thinks it's okay to purchase children to clean your mansion. You make me sick."

"Adir," Sinay said, but he raised his hand to silence her.

"Is that what's happening at your house, Sinay?" Penelope asked.

Sinay nodded, keeping her eyes on Adir.

"If Miss Joyce is mistreating girls, then we can do something about it," Penelope said, glancing back at Officer Gomez. She was nodding at Adir's uncle as he spoke, her hands perched on her police belt. "Officer Gomez has suspected something's going on at the house for a while now. Why haven't you gone to the police?"

Sinay stared at the floor and pulled her sweater sleeves up slowly, revealing the welts Penelope had noticed when Sinay was washing the dishes. "Miss Joyce said I was gone too long one time and she did this to me. Said it would be worse for me if I ever told on her."

Penelope gazed at the rash and went to touch it. Sinay pulled her arm away at first, but then held it up for Penelope to see. It looked better than it had the day before, but was still red and irritated. "What did she do?"

"Drain cleaner. She made me keep it there for five minutes, because I was five minutes late." Sinay trailed off and her eyes glassed over with tears.

Penelope fought back her own tears, fueled more by anger than pain. She put her arm around Sinay's stiff shoulders, hugging her gently. "Did you see a doctor about this?"

Sinay shook her head.

"You see? That woman is the devil," Adir said, spitting his words.

Officer Gomez stepped inside the stock room and looked at the three of them. "Okay. You want to tell me what is going on here?" She glanced at his arm.

Adir glared at her for a second, then shrugged. "I don't have to."

"You appear injured. Your uncle says you've been sick but refuse to go to the doctor. Did you get shot the other night while fleeing a crime scene?" Officer Gomez's radio sputtered on her waist and she reached down to mute it.

"Adir, I think this lady wants to help us," Sinay said, looking at Penelope.

"Help us?" Adir scoffed. "Yes, she will help us go to jail."

"What were you doing at Christian's the night he was killed? Did you go there and shoot him because he was hurting Sinay?" Penelope asked.

Sinay shook her head furiously. "No, Mr. Christian didn't hurt me. He was very nice to me."

"What were you doing in his apartment, then, Adir?" Penelope asked, glancing at Officer Gomez.

Adir stared at them silently, but Penelope felt he was considering his options.

"Fine. If you're not going to tell me, I'll place you under arrest. We'll sort it out with the detectives back at the station," Officer Gomez said, unhooking her handcuffs from her belt.

"Wait," Sinay said. "Please don't. It's my fault. I don't want Adir to get into trouble."

"Sinay, don't," Adir warned, his face softening as he looked into her eyes.

"Adir, we're going to trust her," she said.

She slipped out of the door of the stockroom and over to her laundry cart, pulling a few bags of dirty clothes off of it and digging out a shoebox underneath. She came back to the stockroom and handed it to Penelope.

"What's this?" Penelope asked, pulling off the lid.

"This was in Miss Joyce's suitcase. I unpacked it when she got back from her trip. She's planning on bringing over a new group of girls from Venezuela, where she got me."

"How do you know this?" Penelope asked.

"Look at the pictures," Sinay said.

Penelope pulled a stack of Polaroids from the box.

"That's my sister," Sinay said quietly.

"How does she bring them over here without anyone asking questions?" Penelope asked.

Sinay reached into the box and pulled out a document, holding it up for Penelope to see. It looked like a handwritten invoice, but it listed descriptions for five girls, including names and ages. For each girl there was what looked like an adoption agreement, signed by Joyce Alves.

"What is all of this?" Officer Gomez asked, stepping closer to look at the papers. Penelope filled Officer Gomez in on what she had found out and her trip down to Mrs. Sotheby's basement.

"It looks like she's pretending to adopt these girls," Penelope said.

"But when they get here, she sells them as servants to wealthy clients," Adir said. "They pay a fee and then they get a nanny or a housekeeper. They treat the girls like slaves."

Penelope's stomach did a slow turn. She thought about the burns on Sinay's arms and turned to Officer Gomez. "There, you have proof now. Call for backup and arrest her."

Officer Gomez thought for a second then asked Sinay, "Is there anyone being held in the basement right now?"

Sinay shook her head sadly. "She found work for the last girl yesterday. But she told me to clean the basement, wash the towels and sheets." She nodded towards the laundry cart. "The new girls on that list are supposed to arrive tonight. Please, you can't let her hurt my sister."

Officer Gomez sighed. "This is good. With this it's possible I can get a warrant to search the house, hopefully find more evidence."

"What else do you need to arrest her?" Penelope said, pointing at the paperwork.

"This is a start, but to really make the best case against her, make sure she doesn't walk out the next day for something minor like assault, it would be better to catch her with a victim or making a transaction. She's abused Sinay, but if she's really adopting and selling off young girls, I want to have iron clad proof of that when I arrest her."

"How do the clients know to get the girls from Miss Joyce?" Penelope asked.

"I don't know how they find out. Probably from each other, by word of mouth," Sinay said. "But I know they use a system. Miss Joyce calls them her Blue Card Clients. If they mention they got a blue card from someone, she'll know one of her clients referred them to purchase a girl."

Penelope looked back down at the names of the girls on the paper.

"Denise, what if I go in there and pretend to buy a girl for Arlena? Joyce knows I'm on her staff. I'll say we need help around the house." She looked hopefully at Officer Gomez.

"That's pretty risky. We should call this in and have the detectives send over an undercover unit to do that."

"Gomez," Penelope said. "You've suspected this woman of doing something illegal for a long time, but no one believed you. You're the one who said someone in your department might be protecting her. We can't let anyone else fall victim to Joyce Alves because someone is tipping her off."

Officer Gomez looked at her. "Even if that's true, I can't send a civilian into a dangerous situation."

"Pretend I didn't say anything, then. I'm just going to talk to her, like I did before," Penelope said quickly. "Joyce is by herself in the house now that Christian is gone. She's met me with Arlena already...she's going to trust me more than someone she's never met before."

"Still, I don't think—" Officer Gomez began.

"I have a better chance at not making her suspicious, Denise," Penelope insisted.

"I would like to take her down," Officer Gomez said warily. "I can't stop you from talking to her, obviously. I also can't endorse you doing it either. I'm advising you not to do it."

Penelope's shoulders caved and she shook her head.

"But if I was going to talk to her," Officer Gomez said, looking away from Penelope, "I'd bring up the subject of getting a house girl, but I wouldn't get in her face about it. And I'd get out of there immediately if I felt at all threatened."

"I will, I promise," Penelope said, relieved.

"I didn't hear that," Officer Gomez said. "But I'll be waiting outside, taking my break."

Sinay hugged Penelope, which took her by surprise.

Penelope looked at Adir and said, "You still haven't said why you were in Christian's apartment the night he was murdered."

"We're running away," Adir said. "We knew he had cash and drugs up there, and we could use all of that money to escape."

Adir stood up and pushed a box aside on the top shelf of the metal storage rack, exposing a small duffle bag. He pulled it down and handed it to Penelope. She recognized it as the one she had seen that night bouncing off of Adir's hip as she lay on the patio.

Penelope unzipped the bag and saw a pile of money and two diamond-studded dog collars inside, the ones Max and Christian wore the night Christian was killed.

"Unfortunately this puts you at the scene of a murder, and I can now arrest you for robbery," Officer Gomez said, looking into the bag.

"He was dead when I got there. I didn't kill anyone. We just wanted to get away, start over somewhere together," Adir said. He alternated between sweat and shivers in his jacket.

"Where were the dog collars?" Penelope asked.

"They were just sitting out on the counter. I had to search for the other stuff," Adir said, shrugging.

"Let me look at your arm," Officer Gomez said.

He pulled his jacket off and hiked up the sleeve of his t-shirt. An ace bandage, drenched in dried brown blood, was wrapped around his bicep.

"Yep, you got shot," Officer Gomez said. "And it looks infected. You need to get to the hospital."

"I'm going with him," Sinay said.

"If you're going with him and not going back to Miss Joyce's, I should talk to her now. Can you arrest her if she makes the deal with me?" Penelope asked.

"It would be better if the girls were already here. We'll have her for sure if the hand-off is actually made."

"I will go back and wait," Sinay said. "Miss Joyce won't be home tonight. She's going to a show. I can go to the hospital with Adir and she won't notice."

"Then we'll do the deal with her tomorrow," Penelope said.

CHAPTER 32

Penelope knocked on Mrs. Sotheby's front door a few minutes later.

"There you are," Mrs. Sotheby said. "I wondered what on earth could have happened to you."

"I'm sorry," Penelope said, stepping inside the foyer. "I ran into someone outside. I have to get going, but I may have an idea of what's been going on next door. Hopefully after tomorrow it won't be happening anymore."

"Well, that's exciting," Mrs. Sotheby said. "Anything I can do to help?"

"Maybe," Penelope said. "Will you be home tomorrow afternoon?"

"Yes, I'll be here for most of the day."

"Great. I have something in mind. See you then."

Penelope hailed a cab on the avenue and dialed Joey's number. It rang several times before going to voicemail.

"Joey, hi, it's me. I found the guy from the other night. The one you...you know, hit. He's cooperating with the police. Can you call me back? I hope this makes things easier for you at work. Love you."

She hung up and tapped Arlena's number.

Arlena picked up after the first ring. "Pen, where are you?"

"I just figured out part of what happened at Christian's the other night. Unfortunately, it's not enough to clear Max of murder, but I feel like I'm getting closer. Where are you?"

"I'm in a bistro near Hannah's building. I haven't seen the little witch yet."

"Okay, stay put, I'm heading your way."

Penelope spotted Arlena in the window of the bistro across the street from Max's building, a half-eaten cheeseburger and fries platter on the table in front of her.

"Hungry, huh?" Penelope asked, eyeing the plate.

"Actually, I'm starving all the time now. I don't know if it's psychological or just something I'm doing to fill the time between bad news reports. I've probably gained ten pounds already."

Penelope looked at her skeptically before changing the subject. Arlena's eyes widened behind her large sunglasses as Penelope told her about her trip to Joyce's and what she had planned for the next day. When she'd finished, Arlena said, "I can't believe what that horrible woman is doing."

"I know," Penelope said. "But Sinay said Christian was nice to her, and they had no reason to kill him. Sinay heard the shots and called her boyfriend after everything had quieted down. Joyce was out of town, so she could use the phone without getting into trouble. Adir came to check on her, then decided to ransack Christian's apartment for getaway money."

Arlena sighed. "It's great you're going to help those girls. But Max is still on the hook for Christian's murder unless we find the truth."

"You haven't heard from Max?" Penelope asked.

Arlena shook her head. "I know he's scared, but he can't just run away. He cares about our family—he wouldn't leave us here to deal with everything. I'm sure he's somewhere cooling off, thinking about everything. He'll come back after he's had some time."

"I hope so," Penelope said. "He can't forfeit a two-million-dollar bond, can he?"

"Of course not," Arlena said. "He would never do that to Daddy."

Penelope gazed at the front door of Max's building. She was so absorbed in her thoughts she almost missed Hannah walking out the front doors.

"There she is," Penelope said.

They stood up from the table and hurried outside, jaywalking across the street and following her down the sidewalk.

Hannah walked toward the corner, hugging a large knit sweater over her small shoulders.

"Hannah," Arlena called from behind.

Hannah's shoulders stiffened but she kept walking, quickening her pace, her slouchy satchel purse bouncing off her hip.

"Hannah, wait," Arlena called again.

Hannah slowed her pace and looked over her shoulder, rolling her eyes when she saw it was Arlena and Penelope. "What?" she asked impatiently. Her hair was tucked up in a knit hat, and she wore large sunglasses that obscured her small face.

"Is there somewhere we can talk?" Arlena asked, glancing at the bookstore windows.

"Talk about what?" Hannah asked.

Arlena looked down at the much shorter girl. "Let's talk about the lies you're telling about my brother."

Hannah twisted her mouth up into a smile and turned on her heel to go.

"Hannah," Penelope said. "We know you're pregnant."

Hannah stopped again, turning back to them. "Do you now? How could you know a thing like that?"

"I saw the positive pregnancy test in Max's bathroom," Penelope said. A few people walked past them, giving them mildly curious glances as they went, but no one stopped.

"You're quite the detective." Hannah laughed. She pulled a pack of cigarettes from her bag and lit one up, smirking at them through the cloud of smoke she blew from her mouth.

"You shouldn't be smoking," Arlena said. "You have to take better care of yourself now."

"See, that's the thing. I don't have to worry about that at all.

Because it's not me who's pregnant," Hannah said, taking another drag. "You're smart, but obviously not smart enough to see what's right in front of you."

Arlena stepped closer to Hannah and stared down at her. "Are you telling everyone Max killed Christian because you're jealous of him and another woman?"

Hannah nonchalantly blew out more smoke. "He made promises to me that he obviously had no intention of keeping. Now he's starting a family with someone else. Good luck to them. We'll see how happily ever after he is after defending himself against a murder charge."

"But I saw you with someone else too," Penelope said. "I saw you making out with Christian in the bathroom of the club the night of the fashion show."

Hannah took another drag of her cigarette and threw it on the sidewalk, crushing it under the toe of her boot. "So? Max is allowed to play the field and I'm not? I thought I'd give Max a taste of his own medicine. A jealous man can't ignore you." She smiled playfully at Penelope. "I saw you go down that hallway, knew you'd be in the bathroom, and would run back to squeal on me to your beloved Madison family. Yeah, he talked about you all the time. I know how close you think they are to you." Hannah eyed Arlena up and down from behind her glasses, stopping for a moment to stare at her waist.

Penelope shook her head and said, "You saw who killed Christian, you were there. Why don't you just tell the truth and end this? Don't you care at all about what happens to Max?"

Hannah glanced away, a momentary flash of guilt crossing her face. "I didn't see anything. I only heard Max and Christian arguing in the living room from the bathroom. I listened at the door to hear what they were saying, but it was only Max saying something about being responsible. Imagine that, talking about responsibility, drunk at three in the morning. Then I heard more shouting and a gunshot. I hid in the bathroom until it was quiet, and then I left. Christian was dead and Max was gone."

"Max wouldn't have left you there if you were in danger," Arlena said.

"That's the thing. You don't know Max as well as you think you do, big sister." She turned and walked away from them, slipping into the crowd of people waiting at the crosswalk.

Arlena and Penelope sat in the café at the bookstore and sipped tea. "That was sort of helpful, but where does that leave Max? It feels like with everything we find out, we're making things more complicated for him, not less."

Angel waved at Penelope as she passed by with a stack of books in her arm.

"That's the lady who saw Max and Sienna together in this store," Penelope said. "She said they seemed intimate."

"They're good friends," Arlena said, once again dismissing the idea.

"Has Sienna returned your call?"

"No, but she's busy. She's wrapping up here and going back to London in about two weeks," Arlena said. "Maybe she switched hotels or something came up and she had to get home earlier. I'll try again to get in touch."

Penelope glanced at the clock on the wall of the café. It was shaped like a coffee urn and the hands were made from two spoons. It was hard to tell exactly, but it looked like it was getting close to four o'clock.

"I have to get to work soon," Penelope said. "It's going to be another long night."

"You haven't slept," Arlena said. "How are you going to make it through another night?"

"I don't know. I'll just have to," Penelope said. She hadn't felt tired until they started talking about how tired she should feel. Exhaustion nipped at the edges of her mind. "I'll drink lots of coffee."

CHAPTER 33

After a surprisingly short night of work, Penelope got back to the hotel a little after one in the morning. The director had gotten what he needed in a few takes and decided the crew needed a break. He hadn't decided if they'd be working the next day for sure, so Penelope and the rest of the crew had to wait to hear from production about their next call time. She took a hot shower, then wiped the steam from the mirror to check out her bruises. The edges had faded to an orange-yellow color. After brushing out her wet hair and slipping into some clean pajamas, Penelope stared at the empty bed, stark white with its comforter pulled tight across, undisturbed.

She thought about Joey, about the last time they were really happy, right here in this room. It had only been a couple of days, but already it felt like a lifetime since she'd seen him. She hadn't heard back from him since she left the message about finding Adir, which left her feeling slightly wounded and desperate to hear his voice. But it also made her a bit angry with him for not being there for her when she really needed him, or acknowledging all she was doing to help him.

She pulled the comforter aside and slipped beneath it, turning off the light and silencing her phone. She was asleep within minutes.

* * *

A series of loud knocks on her hotel room door jarred her from sleep. She sat up in bed, trying to figure out what time it was based on the sliver of sunlight between the blackout curtains. Wiping the sleep from her eyes, she glanced at the clock on the bedside table and saw it was just after nine. The knocking started up again and Penelope shook her head.

"Hang on a second," Penelope said, throwing aside the heavy comforter. She looked through the peephole and saw a familiar face, her heart skipping in her chest.

"Max!" Penelope said, swinging the door open wide. She pulled him inside and hugged him tightly, standing up on her tiptoes to reach around his neck.

"Pen," Max said in a raspy voice. "It's so good to see you."

"Come in," Penelope said, releasing him and stepping aside. "Where have you been?"

She watched Max walk into the room, his tall frame appearing larger than life to her tired eyes.

"I've been around, sorting through some things," Max said.

"Arlena must be so relieved you came back," Penelope said. She sat down on the edge of the bed and Max sat in one of the club chairs.

"I haven't seen her yet." Max's eyes had purple bags under them. He looked completely exhausted.

"Max, you have to tell her, and your dad. They're so worried."

"I know," Max said. "I'm going to head up there in a minute. But I wanted to talk to you first."

"Why?" Penelope asked.

"I need to thank you for trying to help me. I'm sorry I called and got you involved in this mess." Max looked at Penelope's face and winced at her bruised eye. "I put you in danger. You got hurt and it's totally my fault."

"Max, I'm just glad you're okay."

"The thing with Christian...I can't remember everything that happened and it scares me. We'd all had a lot to drink...then I think I was hit from behind. I remember arguing with him and then maybe someone coming to the door. Then all I remember is seeing his dead body. There was no one else in the apartment. I panicked and ran."

"What about Hannah?" Penelope asked.

Max shook his head. "I just don't remember."

"You don't know who killed Christian?"

"No," Max said, a pained expression on his face. "I don't want to think it was Hannah, but I know it wasn't me. I've been walking around trying to get my mind to go back."

"Hannah's got no problem blaming you for the murder," Penelope said. "If you were hit on the head, it's possible you won't ever remember, Max."

"I know, and that's the scariest part. Pen, do you think I could shoot someone and not remember it?" Max propped his elbows on his knees and dropped his head into his hands.

Penelope stood up and walked over to Max and looped her arms around his shoulders. "Of course not. You would never do anything like that, Max."

He became very still and leaned into her, his shoulders tense under his leather jacket. They stayed like that for a few moments before Penelope said, "You need a hot shower and some sleep. You're going to feel better, I promise. I've been looking into some things Christian may have been involved with at that house—"

Max jolted upright, looking at her. "Pen, please don't get mixed up any more with these people. If you get hurt again because of me—"

"Max, I want to help you and Arlena. If I can do something to get you out of trouble, I'm going to do it."

Penelope sat down in the opposite chair. "Look, it's none of my business, but what is going on with you and Sienna?" Penelope asked quietly.

Max looked at her, an ironic smile passing over his lips. "She's a great person and an even greater friend."

"I can see that, but what is happening between you two?"

Max sighed. "We're having a baby."

Penelope sat back in her chair and crossed her arms at her waist. "Congratulations?" she finally said.

Max laughed quietly. "Thanks."

"So Hannah finds out about you and Sienna and tries to get back at you by pinning a murder on you?"

Max's face became very still and his features darkened. "That's what it looks like, doesn't it?"

"Where is Sienna now?" Penelope asked.

"I'm not sure," Max said. "We haven't spoken since the night Christian died."

After Max left, Penelope showered and dressed, then picked up her phone to check her messages. The first one was from Gary in production.

"We've sent out an email to let you know, but I'm also following up with all the department heads. There's been a casting change on the set involving one of the leads, so we're delaying for two days to get the new talent caught up. Check your email for dates and particulars."

Penelope sighed and deleted the voicemail, then pressed her phone back to her ear to listen to the next one.

"Penelope, it's Denise. I've got something for you. Call me when you get this."

Penelope hit the call back option and listened to the phone ring a few times before she heard the familiar "Gomez."

"It's Penelope. What's up?"

"I sat on the house last night. I saw the new delivery come through."

Penelope glanced out of her hotel window in the general direction of Joyce Alves's building. "How many girls?"

"At least three, from what I could see," Officer Gomez said. "A little after two in the morning."

"I'm going to try and get one of them," Penelope said.

"I still think it's too dangerous. If it goes wrong, I could lose my job. Even worse, these children could be in more danger."

"You're not telling me to do it, remember? And if it goes right, we'll help them all escape, and put Joyce away. Isn't it worth a try?" Penelope started gathering up her things and loading them into her purse. She pulled her jacket from the closet. "You know what? You think about it. I'm leaving now. Be there in twenty."

Penelope trotted down Mrs. Sotheby's steps, waving goodbye and pulling the door closed quietly behind her. She ducked around the corner to where Officer Gomez was waiting, leaning up against the building gazing at her phone.

"What were you doing in there?" she asked.

"Just saying hi. And I asked her to keep an eye on the courtyard from upstairs, to call for help if I need it," Penelope said. She tucked her white dress shirt into her black slacks. "How do I look?"

Officer Gomez looked down at her outfit. "Like you're going on a job interview."

"Good," Penelope said. "I was going for professional."

Officer Gomez shook her head. "We have a senior citizen as our surveillance backup and a personal chef as our undercover agent. And me out here with no way to hear what's going on inside. So far this seems like a great plan." She muttered something in Spanish under her breath that Penelope couldn't translate.

"I'm going to record our conversation," Penelope said, pulling her phone out of her jacket pocket. "We're just going to talk. I assume it's not like a convenience store where I swipe my credit card and get to walk out with a child laborer. She's either going to agree to a transaction with me or she's going to act like she doesn't know what I'm talking about."

Officer Gomez nodded, but still seemed unsure. "I saw the girls go in, but I can really nail for trafficking if I catch her in the act of selling one of them. If it doesn't work, I'm calling it in and getting them out, charging her with false imprisonment."

"I'm just worried she'll say she's adopted them and that's their dorm room," Penelope said. "She's got that paperwork. She'll walk out of the station, grab them up and they'll all be gone by morning. She's intimidating to them, remember? I doubt they will say anything against her."

"I know," Officer Gomez said, setting her jaw in a tight line. "Okay, do what you can."

"Right," Penelope said. "Let's see what happens."

After a few more minutes of debate and warnings to be safe, Penelope brushed off her jacket and walked around the corner of the house, past the courtyard and up the stoop, pressing the button to ring MUI. The door buzzed open and she was greeted in the reception area by Joyce, the initial look of expectation on her face falling into disappointment when she saw it was Penelope.

"Oh, it's you. What can I do for you?" Joyce asked with a note of boredom in her voice.

"I'm here on behalf of Arlena," Penelope said. "She's interested in hiring some additional talent from you."

Joyce's expression perked up. "Really? I see. In that case, please take a seat. I'll be with you shortly. I'm just finishing up with another client."

"Okay, I can wait a few minutes," Penelope said. She took a seat in front of the hearth and watched Joyce walk down the hall to the conference room. She thought about going to the kitchen to check on Sinay, but didn't want to agitate Joyce if she caught her back there snooping. Penelope pulled her phone out of her blazer pocket and checked that it was still recording, slipping it back in quickly when she heard the conference door open.

"Thank you. We can get that sorted out for you right away," Joyce said as she led someone back down the hall.

Penelope watched as they walked towards her, catching a glimpse of a tall blond man in the darkened hallway. Penelope kept her face as still as possible when she finally saw his face, recognizing Jesse immediately as he entered the main room. He looked at Penelope and did a quick double take, locking his eyes onto hers and then looking away. When he reached the door he turned to say goodbye to Joyce, shaking her hand firmly.

Joyce led Penelope down the hall to the conference room she and Jesse had just vacated. Penelope took a seat at the table.

"Did Miss Madison decide on the girls for her show? We haven't held the in-person auditions yet," Joyce said.

"No, this is for something else," Penelope said. "Arlena wishes to become a Blue Card client. She was told you could help with that." She crossed her legs and sat back in her chair, forcing her shoulders to relax under her jacket.

Joyce pinched her lips. "And who referred her to the Blue Card program?" Joyce said, eyeing Penelope suspiciously.

"Sienna Wentworth," Penelope said without hesitation, taking a chance that her gamble would pay off. "You know they're dear friends. Sienna recommended she get in touch with you if she needed extra help."

"Where is Arlena?" Joyce asked. "I prefer to deal with clients directly when hiring out talent. We have a standard contract we use, which she will have to sign. No agents."

Penelope nodded. "Can you give her an idea of what you have to offer? And the cost?"

"Have her get in touch, and we'll see what we can work out," Joyce said.

"Arlena is very busy, and she'll be disappointed if I don't come back with the information she asked for. Can you at least give me a ballpark figure? I have to report back to her with at least that much."

"Twenty up front, non-negotiable," Joyce said flatly.

Penelope stood up. "I'll relay the message and get back with you by tomorrow."

Penelope and Officer Gomez sat in Mrs. Sotheby's kitchen and listened to the recording on Penelope's phone while she heated up the kettle for tea.

"She doesn't say anything incriminating," Officer Gomez said. "She doesn't trust you enough."

"I can see why she'd be cautious," Penelope said.

"She could be talking about anything. Even about hiring models, which is her legitimate business," Officer Gomez said, turning off the recording. "It was a nice try, but this isn't enough."

"I saw someone I knew in there," Penelope said. "One of the models from Sienna's show."

"He's probably represented by the agency," Officer Gomez said, leaning back in her chair. She was in her street clothes, her long black hair curling over her shoulders.

"Maybe," Penelope said. "I saw him when I went to talk to Sienna that next day at her hotel suite. He was there with his girlfriend. I woke them all up." Penelope thought back to the girl's legs she saw in the bed. Something tugged at the back of her mind, but she couldn't put her finger on it.

"Okay, it's time to call this in," Officer Gomez said. "I can probably get her for holding the girls in that basement against their will. And for the physical abuse to Sinay, who will be my witness. Hopefully we can get the rest of the charges lined up against her."

"And what if you can't?" Penelope asked. "If Joyce has been doing this for a while, she must be good at getting through the red tape. And she might be getting help from powerful people, like you said."

Officer Gomez rested her gaze on the table. "At least if I go in there and get them out, I know they can't get hurt. Or sold."

"But if you're wrong and they're right back with her the next day, you'll have tipped her off. If someone is helping Joyce from inside the police department, couldn't they cause problems for you...get you transferred away from here or worse?"

Officer Gomez looked at her grimly, and balled her hands into fists on the table.

"Here you go, dears," Mrs. Sotheby said, placing two mugs

down on the table in front of them. Officer Gomez excused herself to step outside and make a call.

"Oh, before I forget, thanks for letting me borrow this," Penelope said after she heard the front door close, pulling a small pistol from her purse and sitting it on the table.

"Was it helpful?" Mrs. Sotheby asked, sitting down next to her.

"Yes, thanks. Even though it wasn't loaded, I felt better having it with me, just to scare her if she tried anything."

"Go ahead and hang onto it for a little while, if it makes you feel better," Mrs. Sotheby said. Penelope slipped it back into her purse quickly when she heard Officer Gomez coming down the hall.

When Penelope got back to the hotel, she changed into jeans and a sweater and headed upstairs to the Madisons' suite. She was greeted at the door by Randall, who ushered her into the living room. Max was on the couch next to Arlena, and Sienna sat in one of the chairs facing them.

"I'm sorry, am I interrupting?" Penelope asked, stopping short when she saw Arlena's flat expression and the tears on Sienna's cheeks. "I'll come back."

"No," Randall said, "It's okay. Sienna was just telling us about the baby."

Arlena's eyes cut across to Penelope, her mouth twisted into a half smile. "Yes, Sienna was just telling us that she and Max are having a baby together."

"Wow," Penelope said. "That's huge. So Hannah was telling the truth about that."

Sienna looked at her with an alarmed glance, and Max rubbed her shoulder.

"That's why you're drinking ginger tea, and why you got sick the other morning," Penelope said.

"It does help with morning sickness, but not completely," Sienna said, sighing.

"It's just unbelievable," Arlena cut in, "that my little brother has impregnated one of my friends, after all the times I've told him how I feel about him..." She stood up from the couch without finishing her thought, went to the kitchenette, and grabbed a bag of chips, ripping it open. She crunched angrily and leaned on the counter, staring at Max.

"Arlena," Randall said, walking over and putting a hand on her back. "Love happens when we least expect it. And children sometimes grow out of that love."

"Gross, Daddy." Arlena ate another chip. Her mouth full, she mumbled, "You should be very proud. Your son is taking after you in every way." She grabbed the chips and walked into the bedroom, closing the door forcefully behind her. Penelope followed her, leaning inside the room and mumbling, "You okay?"

Arlena nodded and waved her off, and Penelope closed the door quietly.

"I should go," Penelope said. "Congratulations, you guys." She walked to the door and slipped out, leaving the growing Madison clan behind.

Penelope returned to her room, thinking about everything that had happened over the past few days. Max was going to be a father and had been charged with murder, Joey was somewhere else, her current gig was a nightmare, and she was living in a hotel. She set her shoulders and closed her eyes, determined to get things back under control.

Her phone buzzed in her back pocket and her eyes popped open. She smiled when she saw a text from Joey. "Almost back to NYC. Need to see you."

Penelope typed a quick response.

CHAPTER 34

An hour later, Penelope walked into Read It and Weep and found the small travel section, pulling a book from the shelf about Venezuela. She took it to the café and ordered a candy cane latte, taking a seat at one of the empty tables in the corner. She leafed through the pages, stopping to look at the photos of the various mountains and beaches.

"Hi, Penelope," Jimmy said as he approached her table. He had a few paperbacks under his arm. "You're looking better."

"Thanks," Penelope said. She motioned to the chair next to her and he sat down. "Remember when you told me there was something about a morals clause in Max's contract?"

Jimmy nodded. "Yes, it's a pretty standard clause, so I've heard."

"I wonder what the show would do if they found out Hannah was lying to the police about Max being a murderer because she was jealous of him being with another woman."

"Well, I'm no lawyer, but that sounds pretty immoral to me," Jimmy said. He put his stack of books on the table and folded his hands in his lap.

"She's basically admitted it, dared me to tell Max about seeing her and Christian together. She hasn't come out and said anything publicly about hers and Max's relationship," Penelope said.

"She should worry more about lying to the police than what her fans think," Jimmy said. "They don't like that one bit."

"Can you get me upstairs the next time she's home?" Penelope asked.

"I'll do better than that," Jimmy said, standing up from his seat. "Wait here."

Twenty minutes later, Jimmy entered the café, followed by Hannah Devore. She looked contrite, but there was still a glimmer of defiance in her eyes.

"Hannah," Penelope said tightly. "Thanks for coming."

"I didn't have a choice."

Penelope looked at Jimmy as he retook his seat. "She had a choice. She could either come and talk to you, or I could let some folks know about the contraband housekeeping found in her apartment. Hannah's parents are very clear about it. If she's caught with any illegal drugs, she's shipped right back home and into rehab."

"It was just a little weed," Hannah said, rolling her eyes. "One joint."

Jimmy smiled at her. "Still technically illegal, and still something they'd want to know about. So," he glanced at Penelope, "talk."

"Take back what you're saying about Max," Penelope said.

"Why should I?"

"Because it's a lie, and it could ruin his life."

"And why should I care about ruining his life when he has no regard for mine?" Hannah sniffed.

"I know about Sienna and the baby, and I know it must be hurtful for you," Penelope said. "But you can't do this to him just because you're jealous and upset."

Hannah stared her in the eyes. "The old hag can have him. I've moved on. I never loved him anyway. I just don't want to be seen by the whole world as the one who got dumped."

Penelope shook her head and pinched the bridge of her nose. "So this is just about your reputation? Your heart isn't broken over Max and Sienna?"

"No, I really don't care," Hannah said, smiling. "But you

should ask yourself why he's lying and saying that baby is his. Immaculate conceptions don't happen often."

Jimmy chuckled. "I have to get back. See you around, Hannah."

Hannah rolled her eyes at him. "You want me to recant my statement about Max? Fine. I'm sure it will take more than that to get those charges dropped." She stood up and walked away from the table, leaving Penelope more confused about Max than ever.

She sat for a few minutes, staring into space and letting her coffee go cold. Her phone buzzed on the table, bringing her back to reality. She saw Mrs. Sotheby's name on the screen and answered quickly.

"Hello?"

"Penelope, dear," Mrs. Sotheby said in a voice just above a whisper.

"Hi, is everything okay?"

"Yes, well, maybe. Something is going on next door."

Penelope sat up straighter in her chair. "What's happening?"

"I'm not sure. I saw a man going in and out of the upstairs apartment all morning, like he was moving his things in. Do you think that awful woman would have someone new living there so soon?"

"Well, we think she's trafficking children, so that seems minor in comparison," Penelope said.

"You're right about that. But then I'm sure I heard some shouting, and that young man from the bodega stopped by and got into an argument with the new tenant. He was trying to deliver groceries but the man wouldn't let him in."

"Did you call Officer Gomez?"

"Oh!" Mrs. Sotheby cried suddenly. Penelope heard a faint crackling noise over the phone.

"What happened?" Penelope asked, standing up from her chair.

"I just heard a gunshot!"

"Mrs. Sotheby, hang up now and call 911," Penelope said.

"Oh no," Mrs. Sotheby said, suddenly breathing heavily. "Penelope, help me."

Penelope heard the phone receiver drop on the floor and then silence. She grabbed her purse and jacket and bolted towards the door.

CHAPTER 35

Penelope dialed 911 from the back of the cab, giving them Mrs. Sotheby's address.

"What is the nature of the emergency?" the operator asked.

"I don't know. Maybe a heart attack," Penelope said. "Please hurry, she's there by herself."

A few minutes later the cab pulled up outside Mrs. Sotheby's, and Penelope was shocked to find she had beaten the ambulance there. She pounded on the front door. "Mrs. Sotheby! It's Penelope!"

When there was no answer, she went around the side of the brownstone to the kitchen door. She tried the knob and it turned freely in her hand. She yanked the door open and ran into the house, taking the main stairs two at a time until she reached the office. She heard the ambulance siren outside just as she found Mrs. Sotheby on the floor next to the desk, her face tinged with blue.

"Mrs. Sotheby," Penelope said, placing her fingers on her neck and finding a faint pulse.

"Emergency medical," someone yelled from downstairs as they knocked on the front door.

Penelope took one last look at her friend, then hurried down the stairs to open the door. "She's up there," Penelope said, stepping aside so the EMTs could get past her. She followed them up the stairs and stood in the doorway of the office as they knelt on the floor, assessing Mrs. Sotheby. Penelope closed her eyes and said a quick prayer, fighting back tears as they lifted her onto a gurney and wheeled her downstairs to the ambulance. One of the EMTs handed her a card. "We're taking her to Chelsea Med."

Penelope took the card and nodded. She watched numbly as they lifted Mrs. Sotheby inside the ambulance, closed the doors, and sped away, siren blaring. Penelope's hands started shaking as the shock began to wear off and she headed back upstairs.

She looked down at the courtyard, at the side entrance to Christian's apartment and the padlocked storm doors leading to the basement. Remembering the sound of gunshots over the phone, she scanned the patio but didn't see anything out of place, no evidence of a struggle or fight. Anger burned through her chest as she stared at the house that had caused so much misery for herself, her friends and who knew how many innocent children. She pulled her phone from her pocket and called Officer Gomez.

When she answered, Penelope filled her in on what happened to Mrs. Sotheby.

"I'm in the neighborhood, I'll check in with the hospital," Officer Gomez said.

"She called me about hearing..." Penelope trailed off.

"Penelope?" Officer Gomez asked after she'd gone silent. "You there?"

"Yeah," Penelope said, looking down into the courtyard. She watched Jesse enter through the gates, slinging an empty duffle bag over his shoulder. "Something is going on next door."

"What?"

"I'm not sure," Penelope said. She reached down and touched her purse on the desk, feeling the outline of the pistol underneath the leather, thinking about what Mrs. Sotheby said about hearing a gunshot. She watched Jesse pull open the side door and push his way inside, disappearing up the stairs. "The model I told you about, the one who was talking with Joyce this morning, is going up to Christian's apartment."

"Maybe he's the new club promoter. Christian's replacement."

"Maybe. He knows me. Maybe I can get inside and look around some more," Penelope said.

"Penelope, don't," Officer Gomez warned. "I'm in the neighborhood if you need—"

"I'm just going to say I'm there to follow up on the models for Arlena," Penelope interrupted. "I'll be fine. Gotta go."

"Watch your back," Officer Gomez warned as Penelope hung up.

A few minutes later, Penelope pressed the buzzer at MUI, peering in through the glass doors. When no one answered, she twisted the knob, but it was locked. She pressed the buzzer again, longer this time.

Jesse came in through the main room with an irritated look on his face, which relented somewhat when he saw it was Penelope at the door. He leaned out, his hand loose on the doorknob. "Yes?"

"Hi," Penelope said, taking a quick glance over his shoulder. "Jesse, right?"

He nodded tersely, pressing his lips together, silently urging her to state her business.

"I'm here to follow up with Joyce. My employer is hiring some models."

"Right," Jesse said. "She's not here right now, so you'll have to come back later." He began to close the door.

"Where is she? Do you know if she'll be here? Because I can wait," Penelope said quickly.

"I'm not sure how long she's going to be. Probably a while, so..." Jesse looked over her shoulder someone walking past on the sidewalk, then back at Penelope.

"Do you work for Joyce now?" Penelope asked quickly. "Signed with the agency?"

Jesse shook his head, then began to nod slowly. "Yes, I'm one of hers now. They had an opening."

Penelope cut her eyes towards the courtyard. "You're taking Christian's place?"

Jesse stepped back and opened the door wider. "You know

about a lot of things around here," he said with a faint smile. "You ask a lot of questions, I guess that's why." He began to close the door again.

"Wait, I'd like to leave a note for Joyce," Penelope asked quickly.

"You can just tell me the message and I'll make sure she gets it," Jesse said, becoming more irritated.

"No," Penelope said forcefully. "It's confidential...from my boss."

Jesse's face tightened but he didn't lose his smile. "Sure, come in," he said, stepping aside.

Penelope went to the front desk and jotted something down on a pad of paper, then ripped it off. "Where is everyone today?"

Jesse raised his palms upward and shrugged his shoulders. His shirt cuff rose up and Penelope saw the tattoo on his wrist, and something clicked together in her mind. "Is that Venezuela?" she asked, nodding at his arm.

He looked down at the tattoo and back up at Penelope. "Yeah."

"Are you from there?" Penelope asked, her heartbeat quickening.

"I am," Jesse said. "But I don't remember it. I've been here since I was a child. Do you need anything else, because I should get back to work." He nodded towards the front door.

"Water," Penelope said, faking a cough. "I've been in an accident and I have to take my medicine."

Jesse sighed, and his shoulders caved. "Okay," he said finally. "Wait here, I'll get some."

"Thanks," Penelope said. She watched him push his way into the kitchen and hurried to the door after it swung closed, following him inside.

Jesse stood up straight in front of the refrigerator, a bottle of water in his hand.

"I was hoping to get a couple of crackers too, if that's okay. My medicine makes me sick if I don't eat," Penelope said, laughing a little. "Sorry to be a bother."

Jesse shook his head and handed her the water bottle. He turned toward the cabinets and began pulling them open one by one.

Penelope's eyes flicked to the basement door and saw the padlock was undone, just hanging loosely on the latch. She looked at Jesse's back and then down at the floor where she saw the duffle bag he had been carrying earlier.

"Here, I found some crackers," Jesse said, turning back around. He followed Penelope's gaze, then put the box of crackers on the table.

"Thanks," Penelope said, taking a step closer to the bag. When she first saw the dark blue canvas bag over Jesse's shoulder from across the courtyard it appeared empty, but it definitely wasn't now. "You moving in upstairs?" Penelope asked, attempting to keep her voice casual.

"No," Jesse said quickly, then changed his answer. "Yes, actually. I wasn't going to at first, but it's a great apartment."

Penelope's mind skipped back to the blood on the floor upstairs and she shivered inside. She looked again at the bag on the floor and noticed a red spot on the side, which appeared to be growing.

"Thanks for the water," Penelope stammered, taking a step backwards towards the kitchen door. She felt the weight of the unloaded gun in her purse pulling on her shoulder. Jesse looked down at the duffle bag, then back up into Penelope's eyes. She saw his expression harden, and then he lunged for her.

Penelope spun around and pushed through the door, bumping her injured wrist. She called out in pain and ran, hearing Jesse right behind her. Right as she got to the front door, he grabbed her from behind in a bear hug.

"Where do you think you're going?" Jesse hissed in her ear.

"Let me go," Penelope said sternly, refusing to allow fear into her voice.

"I don't think so," Jesse said, pulling her back from the door. Penelope braced herself against him and tried to twist away. He reached down and grabbed her wrist, squeezing it in his hand. Penelope yelped in pain then cried, "Help!" to the empty sidewalk. Jesse wrenched her around to face him, still holding onto her injured arm.

"You're nosy, and you don't take hints very well," Jesse said, looking down at her wrist.

"You're the one who pushed me?" Penelope asked.

"And yet here you are, still poking around in things that don't concern you," Jesse said. He yanked her closer so their faces were almost touching. "You've seen way too much, and now—"

His expression turned to surprised pain as Penelope stomped as hard as she could with her boot down onto his foot. He stumbled away from her, howling in pain, trying to raise his foot up to his hands. Penelope fumbled with the doorknob and finally got outside, skittering down the steps on wobbly legs. She looked up and down the empty sidewalk.

Jesse tackled her from behind, pushing her down to the sidewalk. She skinned her hands on the cold pavement blocking her face from the impact.

"Get off! Help!" Penelope shouted, hearing her voice bounce off the building across the street, the steel gray windows hiding everything behind them.

"Shut up," Jesse demanded, hauling her up from the ground. He pulled her towards a parked car on the street, once again by her injured arm. Her hand had gone almost totally numb from the pain. "Get in," he demanded when they reached the car, reaching into his pocket for his keys with one hand and popping open the truck. He released her wrist and pushed her square in the back towards the rear of the car.

The feel of his hands on her back ignited a rage in Penelope, the image of the yellow cab approaching the intersection dancing before her eyes. She turned towards Jesse and reared back, shoving him away from her with both hands, using all of her strength. Stars of pain shot through her vision, but she ignored it and charged toward him, pushing him again. Jesse lost his footing and fell against the side of the brownstone, twisting awkwardly and hitting his head on the concrete. Penelope reached into her purse and pulled out Mr. Sotheby's antique gun, aiming it at Jesse while holding her numb hand up against her chest.

Penelope heard a car pull up on the street behind her and a familiar voice say, "Penelope, what's going on?" Officer Gomez spoke with calm urgency. "Let me have the gun." She stepped towards them carefully, glancing from Penelope to the trunk to Jesse, who was pulling himself up to a seated position on the sidewalk, dazed, blood dripping from his forehead.

Penelope handed Officer Gomez the gun. "It's not loaded. He tried to stuff me in the trunk," Penelope said shakily. "And there's a bag in the kitchen with a body in it. Where are the girls?" she shouted at him.

"They're free. Sinay took them up to the bodega to wait for me. I'm going to make sure they're all safe," Jesse said in a daze. "No one helped me, but I'm helping them get away."

Officer Gomez's eyes widened, and she tucked Mr. Sotheby's gun into her belt at the small of her back. She handcuffed Jesse, who offered no resistance, and eyed the cut on his forehead as she called for an ambulance and backup. She pulled him to his feet and sat him in the backseat of her patrol car. He laid his head back against the seat and closed his eyes.

"You said there's a body inside?" Officer Gomez said, gazing up at the brownstone.

"Yes, it's Joyce," Penelope said. "Jesse's got a tattoo of Venezuela on his wrist. I saw it at the hotel suite, but I didn't know what it was until I saw a map of the country and the colors of the flag at the bookstore. Jesse might be one of her victims."

CHAPTER 36

Mrs. Sotheby's eyes opened wide and Penelope smiled at her from the chair in her hospital room. Nurse Kurtz was there too, checking her vitals and adjusting the pillow under her head.

"Penelope, what are you doing here?" She sat up in bed and pulled her hospital gown closer to her neck.

"I hope it's okay. I wanted to check on you to see how you were feeling."

"Oh, of course, dear. I must look a fright though," Mrs. Sotheby said, patting her hair with her fingers.

"You look wonderful," Penelope said. "A lot happened next door this afternoon."

Nurse Kurtz caught her eye and shook her head. Penelope had been warned by the doctor not to talk about the events that led up to Mrs. Sotheby's episode, or about anything that happened afterwards. They didn't want to cause her any stress or excitement until they determined how her heart was doing.

"We'll talk about it later. I just want you to know things should be a lot quieter on your street from now on."

"I can't wait to hear all about it," Mrs. Sotheby said.

"Okay," Nurse Kurtz said. "Visiting hours are over, and the patient needs her rest. You can come back tomorrow."

Penelope stood up. "Please call me if you need anything."

"Thank you, dear. I will."

* * *

Penelope leaned on the edge of a planter outside the hospital, her wrist wrapped in an ice pack Nurse Kurtz gave her after hearing about her tussle with Jesse. She was lost in thought, watching the traffic on the street and the people coming and going from the main hospital entrance. She didn't see him at first, but finally registered that Joey was walking towards her. Penelope blinked and looked again, watching him walk quickly up the sidewalk.

"Penelope," Joey said. His face a mix of concern and relief, he grabbed her up in his arms and hugged her gently, then pulled her away and looked at her bruised face. "I'm so sorry. I shouldn't have taken off on you like that." He looked down at her iced wrist.

"Where were you?" Penelope asked.

"My cousin's hunting cabin in the middle of nowhere. But I don't want to leave you ever again, if I'm not too late." Joey knelt down and gently raised her wrist to get a better look.

"It's not too late for me," Penelope said, fighting the urge to tear up. "When you were gone I realized I've come to rely on you, Joey. If that's not something you're ready for, this would be a good time to let me know."

A pained look crossed Joey's face as he stood up and hugged her again. "No. That's the last thing I want. I've never felt about anyone the way I feel about you, Penny. I was jealous and acted recklessly at exactly the wrong time. I hope you can forgive me."

Penelope leaned into him, closing her eyes and breathing in the familiar scent of his leather jacket. "Jealous of what?"

"Of Max. I see how he looks at you," Joey said, rubbing her back lightly. "I felt like you were choosing him over me that night at the hotel."

"Joey, Max flirts with everyone. Besides, he's going to be a father. That should take up some of his time, clip his wings a little. And I choose you. I have no interest in anyone else. I love you."

Joey pulled out of the hug and held her at arm's length, his eyes glassy. "Max is going to be a father?"

Penelope laughed and pulled him close again, resting her head on his chest. "Yes. I'll tell you about it later."

CHAPTER 37

Jimmy leaned out of the doorway of Max's building and smiled at Penelope. "You're looking much better."

"The bruises are gone, and look," she raised her hand up and moved her wrist around in a circle, "almost one hundred percent movement back."

"Lucky for you, in your line of work," Jimmy said. He reached up and touched his earpiece, listening to a tinny voice for a second. "You here to see Max?"

"Yes, he asked me to stop by. It's my last day on set here, so I was in the neighborhood."

"Come in," Jimmy said, ushering her inside and pulling the door closed behind her.

Penelope walked through the white marbled lobby, admiring the tall Christmas tree in the corner and the red bunting hung on the wall. A menorah sat in the opposite corner, and a large wreath was hung over the elevators.

Jimmy took his seat behind the desk and Penelope signed the ledger, her eyes catching on an entry halfway down the page. Sienna Wentworth had visited Max earlier that morning.

"I have to thank you for everything you helped me with," Penelope said, laying down the pen and looking at him.

"Anytime. I'm glad everything turned out for Mr. Max," Jimmy said, leaning back in his chair. "He's a good guy. No one deserves to be accused of a crime they didn't commit."

Upstairs, Penelope knocked on Max's door. It was opened almost immediately, and Max pulled her inside, wrapping her up in his long arms.

"Pen," Max said, following her into the living room. He clicked off the television and sat down next to her. "Thanks for coming. I wanted to thank you in person for everything you did. I was really in trouble and you stood by me. I don't know how I'm going to repay you for that."

Penelope shook her head. "I don't expect you to repay me, Max. But for your family's sake, just take care of yourself and stay out of trouble. Especially with a baby on the way."

Max stood up and went to the kitchen, returning with two glasses of wine. Penelope accepted hers gratefully.

Max relaxed back onto the couch. "Yes, that's true."

"How do you feel about such a big commitment, Max?" Penelope asked.

Max gazed out at the city lights through the picture window on the back wall. It was getting dark, but the city still buzzed. "I don't know. Fine, I guess."

"Seriously, Max. I thought you'd have more to say than that," Penelope urged.

"Sienna is on her way back to England tonight," Max said. "I'm not sure when we'll see each other again."

"Did you break up?"

"You can't break up when you were never together," Max said.

"Don't you want to be involved in your child's life?"

"I'll be involved, from afar. Now that things have settled down, Sienna is okay again, and capable of taking care of herself, financially and otherwise."

"Max, it's none of my business, and you don't have to say, but when Arlena and I asked Hannah about the baby, she said it wasn't yours."

Max leaned forward and set down his wineglass. He paused for a moment. "I agreed to say the baby is mine. But it's really Christian's."

Penelope's heart skipped a beat. "Christian's? How can that be?"

Max looked at her, a small smile playing at his lips.

"Stop. I know how it could be...but how could it really be Christian's? She acted like she barely knew him when I talked to her."

"It was obviously unplanned, a total fling. And Christian was...let's just say she wasn't thrilled by the prospect of having him in her life permanently. When she found out about his drug connections, she really didn't want to be involved with him anymore, definitely didn't want to bring a child into that kind of lifestyle. She said he'd gotten rough with her once, and she was afraid, but I don't know how true that is, I never saw it. He definitely wasn't interested in settling down, either. He wasn't even interested in seeing Sienna exclusively. When she realized she was pregnant, Sienna came over here really upset, asking for advice on what to do. I didn't know the whole story then, or why she was so anxious about things, but we came up with the idea of saying it was my baby, which calmed her down."

"So that's why Jesse killed Christian? Was he jealous or something?" Penelope said, thinking back to the time she saw them together at the hotel suite.

Max shook his head. "No. Jesse told Sienna what was going on over at the agency. I just found out myself. I had no idea Christian was into something so...disgusting." Max's voice was flat, a big difference from his usually jovial tone. "Sienna just told us all of this when she came to talk to Arlena and Dad about the baby."

"Well, when did she find out? She could have helped do something," Penelope said.

"She did. Sienna says she found out the day before the fashion show, when she went over to bring the final payment to Joyce for all of Christian's fittings and work on the show. Christian told her if she needed any other type of help around the house to ask Joyce and she'd be able to provide inexpensive labor, something odd like that, so she asked. And was totally freaked out about what she was offered in return. She agreed to buy the girls, get whoever she could out of there before they could be sold to someone else. There was only one left, so Sienna took her."

Penelope remembered the girl in the suite, and how protective Sienna and Jesse both seemed towards her. "Why didn't she go to the police?"

"Jesse had her convinced that Joyce had gotten away with it before, that the police were on her side. That's what she said, anyway," Max said, shrugging. "Then Hannah, who is crazier than I realized, walked in on us while I was hugging Sienna, got the wrong idea. Even though she doesn't like me in real life, she didn't want to be embarrassed by me fake breaking up with her on the show."

Penelope's head started to hurt, thinking about everything that had happened.

"All I was trying to do was help my friend with whatever she needed," Max said, picking up his wineglass again and taking a healthy sip, "in a really terrible situation."

"But why? Does Sienna really mean that much to you?" Penelope asked. "It's not like you've been friends your whole life like she and Gavin have."

Max shrugged. "That's the one thing I learned growing up the way I did, with no roots and never staying in one place very long. When you find a good friend, someone important to you who is genuinely a good person, you stick by them. That's what Dad does, you know? He taught me that as a little kid."

Penelope nodded slowly and kept silent. She hadn't thought about Max's upbringing making a difference in his adult friendships, but decided it made sense.

"What about Gavin? What's his part in all of this?" Penelope asked. Gavin was Sienna's longtime fiancé, now ex-fiancé, who had recently come out as gay, effectively ending their engagement.

Max shrugged. "Before she left, she said we could drop the charade. She's an independent woman, and she's going to do it on her own, or with Gavin's help, if he's up for it. I think he will be, they've been close friends forever."

"Seems like you all are, Max," Penelope said. "You were in so much jeopardy because of all of this...I wouldn't blame you for steering clear of them for a while."

"I knew I'd be fine in the end. I have my family, and you, and now I feel like Sienna is part of my family too," Max said sweetly. "You can never go wrong with that many people pulling for you."

Penelope left Max's building a little while later, wishing Jimmy a merry Christmas on her way out. She pulled her scarf closer around her neck and walked towards the bookstore, waving at Angel through the window before slipping inside.

"I've got something for you," Penelope said, pulling a bound script from her messenger bag.

"What's that?" Angel asked, eyeing the dog-eared cover curiously.

"It's an original copy of the script from *Rolling Thunder*. Signed by Randall Madison. Arlena promised you his autograph that day you agreed to help us."

"Oh wow, I forgot about that. This is awesome, thanks!" Angel's face was pink with excitement as she carefully accepted the script from Penelope.

"They're very appreciative of your help, of course," Penelope said. "Merry Christmas."

A few minutes later Penelope left, gingerbread latte in her hand, slipping into the crowd rushing down the sidewalk.

CHAPTER 38

Penelope knocked on Mrs. Sotheby's door, balancing a covered plate in her hand.

"There you are, I was getting worried," Mrs. Sotheby said, pulling the door open wide. "Where is Joey?"

Penelope looked behind her down the stoop. "He'll be right up. He's trying to find a spot."

"Here, come inside," Mrs. Sotheby said, looking up at the falling snowflakes.

Penelope dusted the snow from her jacket and handed the dish to Mrs. Sotheby.

"What's this?"

"A wreath cake. A chocolate Bundt that I decorated," Penelope said. "I'm not the best baker, but I can make a few things."

"Look who I found outside," Joey said. Officer Gomez and Joey came in together.

"Everyone come in and let's sit in here by the fire. Sinay, come on out," Mrs. Sotheby said, rubbing her hands together.

Sinay came into the sitting room carrying a tea service then took a seat next to Mrs. Sotheby on the settee.

A small Christmas tree twinkled in the corner of the living room, decorated with candy canes and colorful glass balls. Mrs. Sotheby poured the tea.

"How are you, Sinay?" Penelope asked.

"I'm doing fine, thanks," the girl responded shyly.

"Are you and Adir still seeing each other?" Officer Gomez asked, warming her hands on her mug.

She smiled and nodded, blushing and looking off at the fireplace.

Mrs. Sotheby patted her on the leg.

"They're taking it slow, right, dear? Just kids, you know," she said knowingly to Penelope. Joey took her hand, lacing his fingers in hers. "School is the most important thing right now, and Sinay is doing wonderfully."

"I'm glad it worked out that you could stay here with Mrs. Sotheby," Penelope said.

"I'm officially a foster parent. Imagine that," Mrs. Sotheby said, taking a sip of tea. "Would you mind getting my glasses from the office, dear?"

Sinay stood up and left to go upstairs.

"I don't like to bring up all of the ugliness of the past few months around her, you understand," Mrs. Sotheby said. "So tell me the latest."

Officer Gomez leaned forward, putting her tea cup on the table and clearing her throat. "Jesse has confessed to the murders of both Joyce and Christian Alves."

"And they were actually related to each other?" Mrs. Sotheby asked.

Officer Gomez nodded. "He was her great-nephew."

"Jesse was one of the first kids Joyce brought over. She sold him to a family out on Long Island who treated him very badly," Penelope said. "He was locked in a closet of the house, only let out to work and clean until a neighbor called the police and the family was arrested. This was years ago."

"So Joyce brought over both boys and girls?" Penelope asked.

"In the beginning, she did. We only have records of girls in the past few years, but Joyce seemed to be an equal opportunity exploiter of children over the years," Officer Gomez said grimly. "Jesse moved to the city and got hired at a club downtown as a waiter, which is where he met Christian one night. Christian recruited him into his modeling circle, and he started doing the club openings with the other models. One night Christian was talking about his great-aunt Joyce, and Jesse thought maybe it was the same Miss Joyce he remembered, since they had the same last name. He got himself invited to one of Christian's parties at the house to find out."

"It sounds like Christian was his friend. Why would Jesse kill him?" Mrs. Sotheby asked, glancing at the staircase.

"He said he wandered downstairs after everyone had passed out one night and saw Sinay scrubbing the kitchen floor at three in the morning. That confirmed for him that Joyce was still bringing kids over and using them as servants. Jesse says he figured Christian had to be helping her, and how could he not be, being her own family."

"Was Christian helping her with the girls?" Mrs. Sotheby asked in a hushed voice.

"We can't find any evidence of that," Officer Gomez said. "Jesse had lost track of Joyce; she used to operate out of Queens and he was just a little boy the last time he saw her. He said he'd built a happy life here and all of that was behind him. But when he came across Joyce again and saw she was still hurting children, he decided it was a sign to do something about it. He assumed Christian was in on it."

"Why didn't he go to the police?" Joey asked.

"He said he tried that before, had filed reports, but nothing had been done...he thought he should try and do something on his own," Officer Gomez said, shaking her head sadly. "The girls were in the back room of the bodega, like he said they'd be. He'd saved up thousands of dollars from his modeling work, was planning on having them live with him until they could be either reunited with their families, or be here legally on their own. His intentions were good. He just went about things the wrong way, I think."

"You can't really blame him," Mrs. Sotheby said. "Sounds like Jesse had it rough growing up," Mrs. Sotheby said. "It's a shame Christian, if he really had nothing to do with Joyce's side business, had to die. But I still find it difficult to believe he had no idea what was going on downstairs, even if he wasn't working directly with her."

They pondered Jesse's fate silently for a moment. Then Officer Gomez said, "Jesse is cooperating, which will hopefully make the outcome better for him. And the charges against Max Madison were officially dropped when Jesse confessed."

"Whatever happened to the gun?" Penelope asked.

"He threw it in the Hudson, off the edge of the GWB. It's gone," Officer Gomez said. "He didn't go over there intending to kill anyone, says it was a spur of the moment decision to confront Christian, and things got out of hand. We're lucky he didn't shoot Max too."

"Jesse may have had a rough life, but he chose to kill two people, and attempted to kidnap this one, don't forget," Joey said, grasping Penelope's hand. "Maybe Joyce and Christian weren't the greatest examples of humanity in the world, but they were still people."

They fell silent when they heard Sinay's footsteps on the stairs.

Penelope shrugged her coat over her shoulders as they walked down the sidewalk to Joey's truck.

The snow had begun to fall harder and she glanced at the empty brownstone on the other side of the courtyard as they passed by. A "For Sale" sign was propped in the front window. Penelope wondered how long it would take to sell, considering all the terrible things that had happened inside.

Joey held the door open for her and she climbed in, rubbing her hands to warm them as she watched him walk around to the other side. The truck roared to life.

"Where are we headed now?"

Joey looked at her and leaned over for a kiss, holding her gently behind the head and lingering for a few beats.

"I want to go see the tree in Rockefeller Center with you. And then I was thinking we'd head back to Jersey, let someone else cook for us tonight."

"Oh really? Who?"

"You know who. We're heading back to the old neighborhood to see the family." He winked at her as he pulled away from the curb.

SHAWN REILLY SIMMONS

Shawn Reilly Simmons was born in Indiana, grew up in Florida, and began her professional career in New York City as a sales executive after graduating from the University of Maryland with a BA in English. Since then Shawn has worked as a bookstore manager, fiction editor, convention organizer, wine consultant and caterer. She has been on the Board of Directors of Malice Domestic since 2003, and is a founding member of The Dames of Detection. Cooking behind the scenes on movie sets perfectly combined two of her great loves, movies and food, and provides the inspiration for her series.

The Red Carpet Catering Mystery Series
By Shawn Reilly Simmons

MURDER ON A SILVER PLATTER (#1)

MURDER ON THE HALF SHELL (#2)

MURDER ON A DESIGNER DIET (#3)

Available at booksellers nationwide and online

Visit www.henerypress.com for details

Henery Press Mystery Books

And finally, before you go...
Here are a few other mysteries
you might enjoy:

THE SEMESTER OF
OUR DISCONTENT

Cynthia Kuhn

A Lila Maclean Mystery (#1)

English professor Lila Maclean is thrilled about her new job at prestigious Stonedale University, until she finds one of her colleagues dead. She soon learns that everyone, from the chancellor to the detective working the case, believes Lila—or someone she is protecting—may be responsible for the horrific event, so she assigns herself the task of identifying the killer.

More attacks on professors follow, the only connection a curious symbol at each of the crime scenes. Putting her scholarly skills to the test, Lila gathers evidence, but her search is complicated by an unexpected nemesis, a suspicious investigator, and an ominous secret society. Rather than earning an "A" for effort, she receives a threat featuring the mysterious emblem and must act quickly to avoid failing her assignment...and becoming the next victim.

Available at booksellers nationwide and online

Visit www.henerypress.com for details

SHADOW OF DOUBT

Nancy Cole Silverman

A Carol Childs Mystery (#1)

When a top Hollywood Agent is found poisoned in the bathtub of her home suspicion quickly turns to one of her two nieces. But Carol Childs, a reporter for a local talk radio station doesn't believe it. The suspect is her neighbor and friend, and also her primary source for insider industry news. When a media frenzy pits one niece against the other—and the body count starts to rise—Carol knows she must save her friend from being tried in courts of public opinion.

But even the most seasoned reporter can be surprised, and when a Hollywood psychic shows up in Carol's studio one night and warns her there will be more deaths, things take an unexpected turn. Suddenly nobody is above suspicion. Carol must challenge both her friendship and the facts, and the only thing she knows for certain is the killer is still out there and the closer she gets to the truth, the more danger she's in.

Available at booksellers nationwide and online

Visit www.henerypress.com for details

GHOSTWRITER ANONYMOUS
Noreen Wald

A Jake O'Hara Mystery (#1)

With her books sporting other people's names, ghostwriter Jake O'Hara works behind the scenes. But she never expected a séance at a New York apartment to be part of her job. Jake had signed on as a ghostwriter, secretly writing for a grande dame of mystery fiction whose talent died before she did. The author's East Side residence was impressive. But her entourage—from a Mrs. Danvers-like housekeeper to a lurking hypnotherapist—was creepy.

Still, it was all in a day's work, until a killer started going after ghostwriters, and Jake suspected she was chillingly close to the culprit. Attending a séance and asking the dead for spiritual help was one option. Some brilliant sleuthing was another-before Jake's next deadline turns out to be her own funeral.

Available at booksellers nationwide and online

Visit www.henerypress.com for details

MACDEATH

Cindy Brown

An Ivy Meadows Mystery (#1)

Like every actor, Ivy Meadows knows that *Macbeth* is cursed. But she's finally scored her big break, cast as an acrobatic witch in a circus-themed production of *Macbeth* in Phoenix, Arizona. And though it may not be Broadway, nothing can dampen her enthusiasm—not her flying cauldron, too-tight leotard, or carrot-wielding dictator of a director.

But when one of the cast dies on opening night, Ivy is sure the seeming accident is "murder most foul" and that she's the perfect person to solve the crime (after all, she does work part-time in her uncle's detective agency). Undeterred by a poisoned Big Gulp, the threat of being blackballed, and the suddenly too-real curse, Ivy pursues the truth at the risk of her hard-won career—and her life.

Available at booksellers nationwide and online

Visit www.henerypress.com for details